"I'll look like a duck in yellow velvet," Daisy said.

Robert squeezed her hand, sympathetically.

Daisy looked at his hand covering her own. She might love him to the very depths of her soul, but Robert wasn't a till-death-us-do-part kind of man—and when you really loved someone, nothing less would do.

She stood up. "Next time you need a shoulder to cry on, try the *Yellow Pages*, since you're so fond of the color."

"Oh, come on, Daisy," he said. "You wouldn't want me to lie and say that you'll look fabulous in yellow, would you? We're friends. Friends don't have to pretend."

Yes, they were friends. Best friends. And she knew that if she wanted to be a permanent part of Robert's life, that was the way it would have to stay.

Born and raised in Berkshire, England, **Liz Fielding** started writing at the age of twelve when she won a hymn-writing competition at her convent school. After a gap of more years than she is prepared to admit to, during which she worked as a secretary in Africa and the Middle East, got married and had two children, she was finally able to realize her ambition and turn to full-time writing in 1992.

She now lives with her husband, John, in West Wales, surrounded by mystical countryside and romantic, crumbling castles, content to leave the traveling to her grown-up children and keeping in touch with the rest of the world via the Internet.

THE BEST MAN AND
THE BRIDESMAID
Liz Fielding

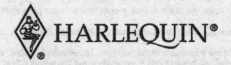

TORONTO • NEW YORK • LONDON
AMSTERDAM • PARIS • SYDNEY • HAMBURG
STOCKHOLM • ATHENS • TOKYO • MILAN • MADRID
PRAGUE • WARSAW • BUDAPEST • AUCKLAND

ISBN 0-373-15870-X

THE BEST MAN AND THE BRIDESMAID

First North American Publication 2000.

Copyright © 2000 by Liz Fielding.

This edition published by arrangement with Harlequin Books S.A.

® and TM are trademarks of the publisher. Trademarks indicated with ® are registered in the United States Patent and Trademark Office, the Canadian Trade Marks Office and in other countries.

Visit us at www.eHarlequin.com

Printed in U.S.A.

CHAPTER ONE

WEDNESDAY, 22 March. Dress fitting. Me, in frills, as a bridesmaid. It's my worst nightmare come true. The self-assertiveness course was a complete waste of time; it was utterly impossible to be assertive in the face of Ginny's sweet pleading. Lunch with Robert first, though. The lovely (and very clever) Janine has dumped him and I am, as usual, the nearest shoulder available. Crocodile tears, of course...but interesting to see how he takes being on the receiving end of the boot for a change.

'Yellow velvet? What's wrong with yellow velvet?'

'Nothing. Probably.' In its place. Wherever that might be.

'If being a bridesmaid was high on my list of ambitions.' It came five hundred and twenty-seventh on hers: right after having her teeth extracted without anaesthetic. 'Nothing, if I enjoyed the idea of being fitted into a dress that will display all my short-comings in the figure department.' She glanced down at her chest, which she suspected would be six inches short of the desired circumference. 'Or, in my case, not display them.' Robert's gaze had followed hers and he was regarding her lack of curves with a thoughtful expression. 'Nothing,' she added quickly, to distract him, 'if I relished the prospect of walking behind a girl who is going to be the prettiest bride this century, alongside a posse of her equally beautiful and raven-haired cousins, all of whom will look ravishing in yellow.'

Was she being petty?

Oh, yes.

'Maybe you'll look ravishing in yellow,' Robert offered. He didn't sound convinced. Well, he didn't have to. Just so long as he stopped talking about Janine. She'd heard quite enough about how wonderful Janine was. If she was that wonderful, he should have married the girl.

Her boyish chest clenched painfully at the thought.

'I'll look like a duck,' she said, more to distract herself than because it mattered very much. It was Ginny's day and no one would be looking at her.

'Probably.' Robert, primed to offer at least a token contradiction, instead grinned broadly. Well, that was why he'd asked her to lunch, to cheer him up.

The best man had it so easy, she thought irritably. Robert would be in morning dress and the biggest decision he'd have to make was whether to wear a grey morning coat or a black one. Or maybe not. Ginny's mother was stage-managing this wedding like the director of some Hollywood epic, and everything was being colour co-ordinated down to the last button, so it was unlikely he'd even have to worry about that.

No. All Robert would have to do was make sure her brother arrived in time for the wedding, produce the rings at the appropriate moment and make a short but witty speech at the reception. She'd seen it all before. Robert was very good at weddings...particularly at ensuring they weren't his own.

He'd arrange a stupendous stag night for Michael and still deliver him immaculately dressed and sober as a judge at the church in plenty of time for the wedding. He'd produce the rings dead on cue, make the wedding guests chuckle appreciatively with his wit and probably have the prettiest bridesmaid for breakfast.

By the time they'd left the church every female heart would be aflutter and the eyelashes would be following suit. Well, not the bride's eyelashes, perhaps. And the bride's mother could be forgiven for being distracted. But the bride's sister, the bride's cousins, the bride's aunts...

Not that Robert needed morning dress for that. Women fell for him wherever he went, whatever he was wearing. Beautiful women. Sophisticated women. Sexy women. And he didn't have to do a damned thing except smile.

Bridesmaids, on the other hand, were at the whim of the bride's mother. She sighed. Frills. Ribbons. Velvet. That was bad enough. But why on earth did Ginny's mother have to choose *yellow* velvet? You'd have thought filling the church with daffodils would be enough yellow for anyone... 'You aren't supposed to agree with me, you know,' she scolded. 'I went to great lengths to avoid being a bridesmaid. I made Ginny swear that no matter what my mother did or said, she wouldn't make me follow her up the aisle.'

'The best-laid plans...'

'The best-laid plans be blowed. I can't believe Ginny's mother permitted such a vital member of her cast to go skiing so close to the wedding.'

'I don't suppose anyone told her about it or she'd have done her best.' He smiled. 'Poor Daisy.' She would do almost anything to have Robert smile at her like that. Even suffer the indignity of yellow velvet. He leaned forward and gently ruffled the springy mop of curls fighting their way out of the confines of an elastic band. 'And actually, you're quite wrong about looking like a duck. Ducks waddle, you don't.' As compliments went, it wouldn't ring a fairground bell, but still Daisy had to work hard to stem a flush of pleasure. 'Definitely not a duck.'

'Really?' The flush materialised; she just couldn't help it.

He grinned. 'No. You're thinking of ducklings.'

Well, that would teach her to be vain. 'Exactly,' she said. '*Fluffy* and yellow.'

'Fluffy and yellow and—'

'Don't even think the word *cute*, Robert.'

'I wouldn't dream of it,' he said, but his eyes betrayed him. Warm, toffee-brown eyes that were quite definitely laughing at her. 'Your nose is too big for cute.'

'Thanks.'

'And your mouth.'

'Okay, I get the picture. I'd crack a mirror at twenty paces—'

'Thirty,' he amended kindly. 'Honestly, I don't know why you're making such a fuss. You'll look sweet.'

Aaargh! 'I'm not cut out for velvet and tulle,' she said tersely. Beautifully tailored suits, severely cut coat dresses and sleek silk shirts were more her style; they flattered her wide shoulders and disguised her lack of curves. 'I certainly don't want to stuff my feet into a pair of satin Mary Janes and have rosebuds entwined in my hair. I'll look about six years old.'

'What are Mary Janes?'

'Those little-girl shoes with the strap over the instep. Why grown women wear them beats me; I hated them even when I *was* a little girl.'

'Oh, I see.' She waited, knowing there was more. 'I have to agree, six does sound about right.'

'Robert!' Well, a girl could only take so much.

He caught her hand, held it, and Daisy decided that he could insult her all day if he just kept doing that. 'Heavens, you're trembling. I've never seen you in such a state.' The trembling had nothing whatever to do with being a bridesmaid, but hey... 'This isn't compulsory, sweetheart. Just tell Ginny that you can't do it.' As if. 'She can manage with three little maids, can't she?'

Of course she could. But this wasn't about managing. This was about having the perfect wedding, and Daisy couldn't, wouldn't let her future sister-in-law down. And there just wasn't anyone else. She'd asked.

Robert, of course, could not be expected to understand. All his life people had been falling over themselves to let him do whatever he wanted. Most men with his advantages would be absolute monsters, she knew. That apart from being the most desirable man she was ever likely to meet he was also good-natured and generous and legions of his abandoned girlfriends would declare with their dying breath that he was the kindest man in the world was little short of a miracle.

'Of course my mother is over the moon,'

she said. 'She didn't expect to get a second chance.'

Robert squeezed her hand sympathetically. 'If your mother wants you to be a bridesmaid, sweetheart, you might as well surrender gracefully.'

If? That was the understatement of the year. Her mother had an agenda all her own. With one daughter married and doing her duty in the grandchildren department, and with her son about to follow suit, Margaret Galbraith already had her sights firmly fixed on her difficult youngest child. Twenty-four and not an eligible suitor in sight.

Phase one of her mother's plan involved getting Daisy to change her image. She was thinking *feminine*, she was thinking *pretty*. She'd already spent weeks trying to involve her in a clothes-buying sortie to take advantage of a large and fancy wedding at which there would undoubtedly be a number of eligible males. Now one of the raven-haired bridesmaids had thoughtfully broken her leg, showing off on the *piste*, and with Daisy the only possible replacement, her mother was in seventh heaven. There was absolutely no chance of escape.

Phases two and three would undoubtedly

involve a major make-up job and the services of a hairdresser with orders to get her fluffy yellow hair under control for once. Daisy sincerely pitied the poor soul who was confronted by that hopeless task.

She looked at Robert's hand, covering her own. He had beautiful hands, with long, slender fingers; a jagged scar along the knuckles only enhanced their strength. He'd got that scar saving her from a vicious dog when she was six years old; she'd loved him even then.

For a moment she allowed herself the simple pleasure of his touch. Just for a moment. Then she withdrew her hand, picked up her glass and swirled the remaining inch of wine about the bowl. 'Mother thinks I'm being silly, that I'm being ridiculously self-conscious,' she admitted. 'She thinks being centre-stage will be good for me.'

He was still smiling, but with sufficient sympathy to put him back in her good books. 'I'm truly sorry for you, Daisy, but I'm afraid you're just going to have to grin and bear it.'

'Would you?'

'Anything for a quiet life,' he assured her. 'But I'll wear a yellow waistcoat to demonstrate solidarity,' he offered, 'if that'll make you feel better.'

'A yellow velvet waistcoat?' she demanded.

'If that's what it takes.' Easy to say. They both knew that unless it was part of the plan, Ginny's mother would veto it. 'Or you could dye your hair black to match the other girls,' he offered. 'Although whether a black duckling would have quite the same appeal—'

'You're not taking this seriously.' But then, when did he ever take anything seriously? He might be a touch aggrieved because his latest girlfriend had worked out that he had a terminal aversion to commitment and cut her losses a full week before he'd made the decision for her, but since he would be beseiged by women eager to take her place, it wouldn't worry him for long.

Daisy sipped her wine in a silent toast to the woman; so few of Robert's conquests were that clever.

'Or you could wear a wig,' he suggested, after a moment.

She told him, in no uncertain terms, where he could stick his wig.

That made him laugh out loud. Well, she had intended it to. 'Don't get your feathers in a tangle, duckie,' he said, teasing her. 'You're getting the whole thing out of proportion. I mean, who'll notice? All eyes will be on the bride. Won't they?'

For a man reputedly capable of charming a girl out of her knickers without lifting more than an eyebrow, Daisy considered that was less than gallant. But then he had always treated her like a younger sister, and what man ever felt the need to be gallant to a sister? Her own brother never had, so why would his best friend be any different? Especially since she went out of her way to keep the relationship on that level. No flirting. No sharp suits or silk shirts when she was meeting him for lunch.

She might love him to the very depths of her soul, but that was a secret shared only with her diary. Robert Furneval wasn't a till-death-us-do-part kind of man, and when you really loved someone nothing less would do.

She downed her claret and stood up. Leaving him on the right note was always difficult; she had to take any chance that offered itself. 'Next time you need a shoulder to cry on, Robert Furneval,' she said, 'try the *Yellow Pages*. Since you're so fond of the colour.'

'Oh, come on, Daisy,' he said, picking up her boxy little beaded handbag from beneath the table and rising to his feet. 'You're the one female I know I can rely on to be sensible.' She might have been placated by that. But then he spoilt it by handing her the bag and saying, 'Except for a tendency to raid your grandmother's wardrobe for dressing up clothes.' She didn't bother to correct him. Her sister had bought her the little Lulu Guinness bag for her birthday, probably egged on by their mother to improve her image. Her image was clearly beyond redemption. 'Don't go all girly on me about some stupid bridesmaid's dress. It's not as if you'll have to show your legs.'

'What have you heard about my legs?' she demanded.

'Nothing. I just happen to remember that you have knobbly knees. I assume that's why you make such a point of keeping them covered up. Trousers, jeans, long skirts...' He smiled down at her with that little-boy smile. His smile did for her every time. Oh, not the knickers. She would never be that stupid. But it still melted every resolve she had ever made in the solitude of her room, still reduced to mush every heart-felt promise she'd made to herself that she would break herself of the Robert Furneval habit. 'You wouldn't

want me to lie and say that you'll look fabulous in yellow? Would you?' It might be
nice, she thought. Just once. But they had
never lied to one another. 'We're friends.
Friends don't have to pretend.'

Yes, they were friends. She clung to that
thought. Robert might not woo her with
roses, might not take her to expensive little
restaurants and ply her with smoked salmon
and truffles, but he didn't dump her after a
couple of months either. They were true
friends. Best friends. And she knew, she had
always known, that if she wanted to be a permanent part of Robert's life, that was the
way it would have to stay.

And she was part of his life. He told her
everything. She knew things about Robert
that she suspected even her brother didn't
know. She had cultivated the habit of listening, and she was always there for him between lovers…to meet for lunch, or as a date
to take to parties. Just so long as she never
fooled herself into hoping that they would be
leaving the party together.

Not that he ever abandoned her. He always
made sure that someone reliable was detailed
to take her home. Reliable and boring and

dull. Then he teased her for weeks afterwards about her new 'boyfriend'.

'Do they?' he persisted.

'What?' She realised he was frowning. 'Oh, pretend? No,' she said quickly, with a reassuring smile. 'I wouldn't ever want you to do that.' She glanced at her watch. 'But now I have to go and submit to the indignity of having the dress taken in.'

'Taken in?'

'The dresses are empire line.' She spread her hands wide and tucked them beneath her inadequate bosom. 'You know, straight out of *Pride and Prejudice*. All the other girls have the appropriate cleavage to show them to advantage.'

'Wear one of those lift 'em up and push 'em together bras,' he suggested.

'You have to have something to lift and push.'

He didn't argue about that, but rubbed his hand absently down the sleeve of her jacket. 'Don't worry about it, Daisy. Everything will be fine. And the wedding will be fun, you'll see.'

She gave him the benefit of a wry smile. 'For you maybe. Best man gets the pick of the bridesmaids, doesn't he?'

He gazed down at her. 'I've never been able to fool you, have I?'

'Never,' she agreed.

'Better cut along to this fitting, then, so that you can give me the low-down on Saturday.'

'Saturday?'

'There's a party at Monty's. I'll pick you up at eight and we'll have dinner first.'

It never seemed to occur to him that she might have something else planned, and for just a moment it was on the tip of her tongue to tell him that she was busy on Saturday night. There was only one problem with that. In all her life, since she was old enough to toddle after her brother and his best friend, she had never been too busy for Robert. 'Make it nine-thirty,' she said, forcing herself to be a little difficult. Just to prove to herself that she could be.

'Nine-thirty?' His dark brows twitched together in gratifying surprise.

'Actually ten o'clock would be better,' she said. 'I'll have to give dinner a miss, I'm afraid.'

'Oh? Are you sure you can manage the party?' The edge in his voice gave Daisy rather more satisfaction than was quite kind.

After all, she'd chosen the path she was treading. 'You haven't gone and got yourself a boyfriend, have you? You're my girl, you know.'

'No, I'm not,' she said, putting on her sweetest smile. 'I'm your friend. Big difference.' His girls lasted two, three months tops, before they started hearing wedding bells and he, with every appearance of reluctance, let them go. 'But I was going to Monty's bash anyway and I'll be glad of the lift.' Just occasionally he needed to be reminded that she wasn't simply there at his beck and call. Just occasionally she needed to remind herself, even if it did mean passing on dinner at some fashionable restaurant and dining alone on a sandwich.

Then, having made a stand, having started a tiny ripple in his smoothly ordered world, she held up her cheek to be kissed, punishing herself with the brief excitement of his lips brushing her cheek, the scrape of his midday beard against her skin that did things to her insides that would rate an X-certificate.

It would be so easy to prolong the hug, just as it would have been easy to indulge herself and stretch out lunch over coffee and dessert. But Daisy's little-sister act had its limitations; too much close contact and she'd be climbing the office walls all afternoon.

Besides, keeping him at a distance was probably the only reason he didn't get bored with her.

'Thanks for lunch, Robert. I'll see you on Saturday,' she said briskly, making for the restaurant door and not looking back once. It had been harder today. Much harder. Today he was unattached, momentarily vulnerable in a way she hadn't seen before. Maybe that was why she had made such a fuss about the bridesmaid dress. Not to amuse Robert, but to distract herself.

It would have been far too easy to forget all about the fitting, to suggest he walk her across the park, linking her arm through his, inviting him up to her flat with the excuse that she wanted to show him her new computer, plying him with coffee and brandy.

The trouble was she knew Robert too well. All his little weaknesses. Today, dumped by a girl with the wit to see through him, with his self-esteem needing a stroke, he might have been tempted to see what Daisy Galbraith was really made of beneath the trousers, the long skirts, the carefully neutral, sexless clothes she wore whenever she met him.

The trouble with that inviting scenario was tomorrow. Or perhaps next week. Or maybe it would be a month or two before someone else, someone elegant and beautiful, someone more his style, caught his roving eye. And after that nothing. No more precious lunches. No more of those early Sunday mornings at home when he dropped by with his rods to suggest they might go fishing, or take the dogs for a run. No more anything but awkwardness when they met by chance.

Worse, she would have to pretend she didn't care, because her brother would never forgive his best friend for breaking his little sister's heart.

While a treacherous part of her mind sometimes suggested that an affair with Robert might be all it took to cure her of his fatal attraction, Daisy had no difficulty in ignoring it. She might be foolish, but she wasn't stupid. She'd been in love with him since she had gazed from her high chair at this seven-year-old god who had come home with her brother for tea. The very last thing on earth she wanted was to be cured.

*   *   *

'More coffee, sir?' Robert shook his head, retrieving his credit card from the plate and, on an impulse, heading quickly for the door, hoping to catch Daisy so that they could walk across the park together. She always walked, but then she always wore good sensible shoes, or, like today, well-fitted laced ankle-boots, even in London. She was so easy to be with. Always had been, even when she was a knobbly kneed kid trailing after him and Michael.

Then he frowned. Yellow? What was wrong with yellow? What was wrong with 'cute'? What was wrong with ducklings, come to that?

From the pavement outside the restaurant he could see her bright froth of hair bobbing along in the distance as she strode across the park, and he realised that he'd left it too late to catch her. Oh, well. He'd see her on Saturday. And as he hailed a cruising cab, he frowned. Ten o'clock? What on earth could she be doing until ten o'clock?

Being stripped to her underwear, with her reflection coming back at her from a terrifying array of mirrors, was doing nothing for Daisy's self-confidence, and she was almost grateful for the covering of yellow velvet despite the fact that it emphasised her own lack of curves.

The seamstress attacked the spare material with a mouthful of pins, tucking it back to fit Daisy's less generous curves. Once satisfied, she nodded. 'All done. Can you come back early next week?'

'I couldn't bribe you to spill something indelible on it, could I? A pot of coffee? A squirt of ink?'

'What's the matter? Don't you like it?' The woman seemed surprised.

'With my colouring? Yellow would not be my first choice.'

'Well, there's a first time for everything.'

'Yes. And a last.'

'It's just different, that's all. With the right make-up you'll make a really pretty bridesmaid.'

Oh, Lord, that, if anything, was worse. Prettiness was her mother's fantasy; she had known better than to attempt it. She certainly didn't want to look as if she were competing with the other bridesmaids.

'Daisy!' Ginny burst through the door with the rest of her adult attendants in tow. Dark, glossy and gorgeous to a girl. Robert was going to have a ball, she thought with that detached part of her brain that dealt with everything Robert did when he was not with her. It was just so much easier when she wasn't part of the show. 'You're early!'

'No, darling, you're late.'

'Are we? Oh, Lord, so we are. We've been having facials,' she giggled. 'You should have come.'

There was more than one way to take that remark, Daisy decided, but was sure that Ginny hadn't meant it unkindly. Ginny didn't have an unkind bone in her body and, while her figure might leave something to be desired, Daisy knew there was nothing wrong with her skin. There was, unfortunately, precious little that a facial could do about an over-large nose or mouth.

She arrived back at her office, breathless and feeling just a bit low. 'Ah, Daisy, there you are.'

Yes, here she was. And here she'd probably be for the rest of her days; Robert's best friend and stand-by date. She pulled herself together; feeling sorry for herself wasn't going to help. 'I'm sorry, George, I did warn you I might be late.'

'Did you?' George Latimer was nearing seventy, and while few could challenge his knowledge of oriental artefacts, his short-term memory was not quite what it might be.

'I had to be pinned into the bridesmaid dress,' she reminded him.

'Ah, yes. And you had lunch with Robert Furneval,' he added thoughtfully. In the act of hanging up her jacket, Daisy turned. She'd said she was lunching with a friend; she hadn't mentioned Robert. 'Your clothes give you away, my dear.'

'Do they?'

'You're covered from neck to ankle in the most unattractive brown tailoring. Tell me, are you afraid that he'll get carried away and seduce you in the restaurant if you wear something even moderately appealing when you meet him? I only ask because I get the impression that most young women would enjoy the experience.'

Her feigned surprise had not fooled him for a minute. His short-term memory might be a touch unreliable, but there was nothing wrong with his eyesight. And noticing things was what made him so good at what he did.

'I didn't realise you knew Robert,' she said, avoiding his question.

'We've met in passing. I know his mother. Charming woman. She's something of an authority on netsuke, as I'm sure you know. When she heard I was looking for an assistant she called me and suggested I take you on.'

Daisy sat down rather quickly. 'I had no idea.' Jennifer Furneval had always been kind to her, taking pity on the skinny teenager who had hung around hoping to be noticed by her son. Not that she'd so much as hinted that she knew the reason why Daisy had developed such a fervent interest in her collection of oriental treasures. On the contrary, she had loaned her books that had been a blissful excuse to return to the house, to hang around, ask questions. And she had eventually pointed her in the direction of a Fine Arts degree.

Of course, she'd stopped hanging around for a glimpse of Robert long before then. She stopped doing that the day she'd seen him kissing Lorraine Summers.

She'd been sixteen, all knees and elbows, an awkward teenager whose curves had refused to develop and with an unruly mop of hair that had repulsed every attempt to straighten it—assaults with her mother's curling tongs leaving her with nothing but frizz and the scent of singed hair to show for her efforts.

Her friends had all been developing into embryonic beauties, young swans while she'd seemed to have got stuck in the cygnet phase. The archetypal ugly duckling. But she hadn't minded too much, because while the swans had made eyes at Robert they'd been far too young to win more than an indulgent smile. Daisy, on the other hand, had kept her eyes to herself, and had never asked for more than to sit and watch him fishing.

Her reward, one blissful summer when Michael had been away on a foreign exchange visit, had been to have Robert give her an old rod and teach her how to use it.

That, and the Christmas kiss he'd given her beneath the mistletoe. It was the best present she'd had that year. The glow of it had lasted until June, when she'd seen him kissing Lorraine Summers and realised there was a lot more to kissing than she'd imagined.

Lorraine had definitely been a swan. Elegant curves, smooth fair hair and with all the poise that a year being 'finished' in France could bestow on a girl. Robert had just come up from Oxford, a first-class honours degree in his pocket, and she had gone racing around there to just say hello. Congratulations. Will you be going fishing on Sunday? But Lorraine, with her designer jeans and painted nails and lipstick, had got there first.

After that she had only gone to see Jennifer Furneval when she'd been sure that Robert was not there.

He had still dropped by, though, when he'd been home. Her brother had been in the States, doing a business course, but Robert had still called in early on a Sunday morning with his mother's dog, or with his rods. Well, he'd always been able to rely upon Daisy to put up some decent sandwiches and bring a flask of fresh coffee, and maybe Lorraine, and the succession of girls who had followed her through the years, hadn't cared to rise at dawn on a Sunday morning for the doubtful honour of getting their feet wet.

'She worries about him, I think,' George Latimer continued, after a moment's reflection.

Daisy dragged herself back from the simple pleasure of a mist-trailed early-morning riverbank to the exotic *Chinoiserie* of the

Latimer Gallery. 'About Robert? Why? He's successful by any standards.'

'I suppose he is. Financially. But, like any mother, she'd like to see him settle down, get married, raise a family.'

'Then she's in for a long wait. Robert has the perfect bachelor existence. A flat in London, an Aston Martin in the garage and any girl he cares to raise an eyebrow at to keep him warm at night. He isn't about to relinquish that for a house in the suburbs, a station wagon and sleepness nights.' Not sleepless nights caused by a colicky baby, anyway.

He didn't argue. 'So that's why you dress down when you have lunch with him?'

Yes, well, she knew George Latimer was sharp. 'We're friends, George. Good friends, and that's the way I plan to keep it. I don't want him to confuse me with one of his girls.'

'I see.'

Daisy wasn't entirely comfortable with the thoughtful manner in which George Latimer was regarding her, so she made a move in the direction of her office, signalling an end to the conversation. 'Shall I organise some tea? Then we can go through that catalogue,' she said, indicating the glossy catalogue for a large country house sale that he was holding, hoping to divert him. 'I imagine that was why you were looking for me?'

He glanced down at it as if he couldn't quite remember where it had come from. 'Oh, yes! There's a fine collection of ceramics up for auction. I'd like you to go to the viewing on Tuesday and check them out.' She felt a rush of pleasure at this token of his trust. 'You know what to look out for. But, since you'll be representing the gallery, I'd be grateful if you'd avoid Robert Furneval while you're there.' He peered over his half-moon spectacles at her. 'Wear that dark red suit, the one with the short skirt,' he elaborated, in case she was in any doubt which one he meant. 'I like that.'

'I didn't realise you took such an interest in what I wear, George.'

'I'm a man. And I like beautiful things. Have you got any very high-heeled shoes to go with it?' he continued before she could do more than retrieve her jaw from the Chinese rug that lay in front of her desk. 'They'd do a fine job of distracting the opposition.'

'I'm shocked, George,' she said. 'That's

the most sexist thing I've ever heard.' Then, 'Actually, I've seen a pair of Jimmy Choo's that I would kill for. Can I charge them to expenses?'

The lenses gleamed back at her. 'Only if you promise to wear them next time Robert Furneval asks you to lunch.'

'Oh, well. It'll just have to be the plain low-heeled courts I bought for comfort, then. Pity.'

CHAPTER TWO

SATURDAY 25 March. I've bought the shoes. Wickedly sexy, wickedly expensive, but I used the money Dad sent me for my birthday. Oh, the temptation to wear them to Monty's party tonight! I would if Robert wasn't going to be there. I wonder if anyone else notices that I dress differently around him? Michael, probably. But then I'm sure that Michael knows the truth and, since he's made no attempt to matchmake, understands why. I'll probably still be filling the 'girlfriend gap' when Robert's heading for his pension. And still be going home alone.

Daisy had plenty of time in which to contemplate her wardrobe and worry about what she should wear to the party. Plenty of time to call herself every kind of idiot, too.

She could have been dining in some exquisite little restaurant with Robert when, for pride's sake, she had chosen a lonely cottage cheese sandwich and the inanity of a

Saturday-night game show on the television. The fact that it was the sensible option did not make it any more palatable.

This was no way to run a life. She switched off the television, abandoned the half-eaten sandwich and confronted her wardrobe. Just because she knew better than to join in the queue for Robert's attention, it didn't mean she shouldn't make the effort to get into some sort of relationship, if only to allay her mother's for once unspoken but nevertheless obvious fears that her interests lay in another direction entirely.

She might not be able to compete with Robert's glamorous 'girls', but her lack of curves didn't appear to totally discourage the opposite sex. Most of the young gallants that Robert had deputised to escort her home from other parties had at least made a token pass at her. One or two had tried a great deal harder. Asking her out, phoning her until she'd had to be quite firm...

Oh, no! He couldn't! He wouldn't! Would he? She flushed with mortification to think that Robert might have encouraged them to be, well, *nice* to her.

Could it be that his only motive in taking her along to parties was to try and match her up with some eligible young male? Was it possible that her mother had asked him to? With a sinking feeling she acknowledged that it was exactly the sort of thing that her mother would do. She could just hear her saying, *Robert, there must be dozens of young men working at your bank. For goodness' sake try and fix Daisy up with someone before she's left on the shelf...*

She knew she should be grateful that her mother had never harboured ambitions for her in Robert's direction. Clearly he was far too glamorous, good-looking, too everything for the plainest member of the family.

She pulled out a pair of wide-legged grey silk trousers. She'd intended to match them with a simple black sweater which was elegant in a rather dull, don't-notice-me sort of way. If she could have been sure that Robert wouldn't be at the party, she would have worn something rather more exciting.

Maybe she should anyway?

After all, if Robert thought she was so unattractive that he pushed his reluctant juniors in her direction, what she wore wasn't going to make a blind bit of difference, was it?

Damn, damn, damn. Why did it have to be so complicated? She just wanted to be his friend. That was all. But you don't patronise friends...

She blinked at eyes that were suddenly stinging, but nothing could stop the tear from spilling down her face. She had tried so hard to be sensible, but she loved him so much. Not like the constant parade of the lovely women who moved through his life. She wasn't in the least bit impressed by the glamorous job in the City, his money, the fast cars, his good looks. She'd love him without any of the fancy trappings because she cared about *him*. She always had. Not because she wanted to. Because she couldn't help it.

She'd hoped that going away to university would have stopped all that. Really hoped that she would meet someone who would make her forget all about Robert. Maybe she hadn't looked hard enough. Maybe, deep down, she hadn't wanted to. But maybe it was time to put a stop to this stupid game she'd been playing. Walk away, before she did something really stupid.

After the wedding, she promised herself, drying her cheek with the heel of her hand.

She'd stop being available. Make herself busier. Take up knitting.

Oh, for heaven's sake! Now she was being

pathetic. Well, she could put a stop to that right now. This minute. Tonight she wouldn't hang around waiting for Robert to remember to dance with her. Tonight she'd pick her own escort home, or at least leave with some dignity on her own.

She looked her reflection straight in the eye and promised herself that if she could sort herself out a date for the wedding, she'd do that, too. It would please her mother, if nothing else. She palmed her eyes, trying to cool them.

Then she blew her nose, stood up and headed for the shower, determined that there would be no dressing down tonight. None of that barely there make-up.

She painted her nails bright red, she sprayed on her scent with reckless abandon, and instead of squeezing her hair into a French plait in order to keep it under control she left it fluffy. It wasn't chic. It wasn't that sleek, glossy stuff that swung and caught the light and looked like a million dollars in the shampoo adverts. In fact all that could be said in its favour was that she did have a heck of a lot of it.

She'd tried cutting it short once, but it hadn't helped. She'd simply looked like a poodle after a less than successful encounter with the clippers. The only thing that had stopped her cutting it to within an inch of her scalp had been the sure and certain knowledge that what remained would curl even tighter, and shaving her head would just have been a temporary solution. Maybe that was the answer now, she thought, grinning as she flattened her curls against her skull with her hands. Not even dear, sweet, kind Ginny would put up with a skinhead as a bridesmaid. Would she?

A brisk ring at the doorbell put a stop to such nonsense. She checked her watch; it was still a quarter of an hour until ten o'clock. He was early, impatient with her delaying tactics, and that was unusual enough to make her smile as she pressed down the intercom.

'You're early.'

'Then I'll have a drink while I wait,' Robert's disembodied voice informed her.

She let him into the building and then opened her flat door before retreating to her bedroom to paint her lips as red as her nails. 'There's wine in the fridge,' she called from the bedroom, staring nervously at her reflection now that he had arrived, wondering if she'd gone a bit too far.

'Shall I pour a glass for you?'

'Mmm,' she said. She definitely needed a drink. Oh, well. In for a penny... She fitted a pair of exotic dangly silver earrings to her lobes and then stepped into the new shoes. They would be wasted, she decided. No one would see them. She stepped out of them again and, like the coward she was, put on a pair of low-heeled pumps.

Robert, tall, square-shouldered, with the fine, muscular elegance of a fencer and utterly gorgeous in pale suit and a dark green shirt, paused in the kitchen doorway as he saw her. Paused for a moment, taking in the wide silk pants, the tiny black and silver top that crossed low over her small breasts like a ballet dancer's practice sweater and tied behind her waist...and said nothing.

He thought she looked like a little girl who'd been caught playing with her mother's make-up, but was too polite to say so; Daisy could see it in his face and wanted to run howling back to the bathroom to scrub her face.

'Have you been somewhere special?' he asked finally, handing her a glass. For a moment she couldn't think what he meant. 'You couldn't make dinner,' he reminded her, eyes narrowed.

'Oh. Um…' She floundered for a moment. 'It was just a gallery thing.' Work. That was it, she decided, clutching at straws. Anything rather than have him think she'd done this to impress him.

'A viewing? I'd have come if I'd known. I'm looking for something for my mother's birthday.'

'Are you? What?' she asked, hoping to divert him further.

'When I see it, I'll know. So? Was it a viewing?' he persisted, refusing to be sidetracked.

'Um… No. Not exactly.' He raised one of his dark, beautifully expressive eyebrows and took a sip of wine without commenting, leaving Daisy with the uncomfortable feeling that he didn't quite believe her. But what else could she say? She refused to own up to staying in and watching television rather than have dinner with him. He wouldn't understand why and she certainly couldn't explain.

'You shouldn't let George Latimer work you so hard,' he said, after a silence that seemed unusually awkward.

'He doesn't,' she snapped back. 'I love my job.' Perhaps it was guilt at lying to him that made her so sharp. She certainly didn't feel capable of the usual easy banter that sustained their conversation. 'Shall we go?'

Robert Furneval reached the pavement and without thinking hailed a passing taxi. 'We could easily have walked,' Daisy said.

'If you've been working, you deserve to ride.' If? What on earth had made him say that? The feeling that she hadn't been quite honest with him? Daisy had looked so guilty when she'd told him that she'd been working late. Guilty and unusually glamorous. If George Latimer had been forty, thirty years younger even, he might have suspected there was something going on.

Ridiculous of course. But being busy until nine-thirty smacked of the kind of affair where the man needed to be home with his wife and children at a respectable time. He glanced across at her, and even in the dim light of the cab he could see that her eyes were very bright. And she'd flushed so guiltily. But Daisy would never have that kind of affair. Would she?

He thought he knew her, yet it occurred to

him that he had no idea what she might do if tempted. What exactly did she do in the evenings when the shutters came down at the gallery?

She never talked about herself much. Or was it that he never asked? No, that wasn't right. He was good at relationships, knew how to talk to women... But he knew Daisy so well. Or thought he did. The girl sitting beside him in the taxi seemed more like a stranger.

He'd always thought of her as Michael's kid sister, always there. Good natured, fun, a girl who didn't make a fuss about getting a bit muddy. But tonight her eyes were shining and her cheeks looked a touch hectic. It was a look that he knew and understood. On Daisy, it made him feel distinctly uncomfortable. Almost as if he had lifted aside a veil and seen something secret.

She turned and caught him looking at her, and for a moment he had a glimpse of something much deeper. Then she cocked a quirky eyebrow at him and grinned. 'What's up, Robert? Still missing the gorgeous Janine?' she teased.

He relaxed. She hadn't changed. He was

the one who was tense. 'Hurt pride, nothing worse,' he admitted.

'You're getting slow. If you're not very careful one of these days you'll find yourself walking down the aisle and you won't be the one behind, flirting with the bridesmaid, you'll be the one in front, with the ring through your nose.'

'That's it, kick a man when he's down.'

'I'll give you half an hour before you're bouncing right back. Tell me, which terribly nice young man are you planning to send me home with tonight?'

'Who said I was planning to send you home with anyone?' he demanded.

'Because you always do. I sometimes think that you must keep a supply of clones handy, to be activated in emergencies.'

'Emergencies?'

She clutched her hands to her heart. 'You know... Fabulous redhead... Let's go on to a club... Duh! What'll I do with Daisy...?' She grinned. 'That kind of emergency.'

'Oh, cruel! For that, miss, I shall take you home myself and—'

'And?'

And what? He might have teased her about boyfriends, but as far as he knew she'd never taken things further than goodnight-and-thank-you with any of the guys he'd deputised to take her home, some of whom had begged him for the privilege. Not that he was going to tell her that. She didn't deserve to be flattered. 'You won't get away with a polite handshake and goodnight with me. I'll expect coffee and a doorstep-sized bacon sandwich for my trouble.'

'How do you know they just get a polite handshake?' she asked archly. 'Do they report back to you?'

'Of course,' he lied. He didn't need to be told, their disappointment was self-evident. 'I want to know that you arrived home safely.'

She grinned. 'And it never occurred to you that they might not be telling the truth?'

'They wouldn't dare lie.'

'Is that right?' She was laughing at him. So that was all right. Wasn't it? 'One day, Robert, you'll come seriously unstuck. But if you can tear yourself away from the first gorgeous redhead who smiles at you, or the first blonde, or brunette, you can have all the coffee and bacon sarnies you can eat. But don't expect me to be holding my breath.'

'Actually, I'm saving myself for the lovely

bridesmaids,' he said, mock seriously. 'You did say they were lovely, didn't you?'

'Stunning. I'll give you a run-down over supper. If you remember.'

'Cat,' he murmured, as the taxi slowed. He climbed out first, and by the time he had paid the driver Daisy was inside, the welcoming crowd parting to swallow her up in its warm embrace. She was, he knew, one of those girls everyone was glad to see. He was always glad to see her, too. He didn't see her often enough.

Someone put a drink in his hand, then he was grabbed by an acquaintance who wanted some free advice about an investment, and he had just been buttonholed by a girl who seemed to know him, but whose name he couldn't remember, when he saw Daisy chatting to a tall, fair-haired man he didn't know. A man who was looking at her in a way that suggested he had only one thing on his mind.

It was a look that aroused all kinds of ridiculous protective male urges in him. 'Excuse me,' he murmured to the blonde, abandoning her and the mental struggle for her name without a second thought.

The man was Australian, lean and suntanned and revoltingly good-looking, and

Daisy was laughing at something he'd said. In fact she looked as if she was having a very good time. That irritated him. She was his date. 'Can I get you a drink, sweetheart?' he said, slipping his arm about her waist.

'No, thanks,' she replied, turning to look at him with some surprise. Justifiable surprise, since he rarely worried about her once they were at a party. After all she knew everyone. Almost everyone. 'Nick's looking after me. Have you met?' she asked. 'Nick, this is Robert Furneval. Robert, Nick Gregson.'

Robert gave the Australian the kind of look that suggested it was time to find someone else to talk to. For a moment he looked right back, then, getting no encouragement to stay from Daisy, he shrugged and disappeared into the crowd.

'What's the matter?' Daisy asked, turning to him. 'Didn't the blonde go for your usual chat-up line?' She raised her voice as someone turned up the music.

He got the impression Daisy wasn't very pleased with him. 'What chat-up line?' he demanded.

'I've no idea, but you must have one. You

can't possibly think up something new to say to every girl you meet.'

'You're very touchy tonight, sweetheart. Is this my payoff for agreeing that you'll look like a duck at Michael and Ginny's wedding?'

'What?'

'For saying that you'll look like a duck...' Unhappily, ''...you'll look like a duck...'' coincided with one of those sudden drops in noise level that occasionally happens in a crowded room, and everyone turned to stare.

Daisy flushed. 'Well, thanks, Robert,' she said. 'I really needed that.' And she placed her glass in his hand and walked away.

Daisy was furious. She couldn't ever remember being angry with Robert before, and the sensation was rather like taking a deep breath over the bottle of smelling salts that her mother used as a reviver on particularly strenuous jaunts around stately homes. A dizzy blast that was a lot more intoxicating than the wine she had been drinking.

Maybe that was why, when her natural circulation of Monty's flat brought her back to the Australian with the sun-bed tan, she was rather more encouraging than she might have been. Especially since Robert was glowering at him rather than giving his full attention to a luscious brunette who quite evidently hadn't learned a thing from her predecessors' mistakes. But then maybe she didn't care about commitment. Robert was *very* good looking.

Nick jerked his head in Robert's direction. 'Are you and he…' He shrugged, leaving her to mentally fill in the gap with whatever relationship she thought appropriate.

She dragged her gaze back from Robert and gave Nick her full attention. 'Robert and me?' She managed a laugh. 'Heavens, no, we're just good friends. I've known him since I was in my cradle. He's more like a brother.'

'Is that right?' He grinned. Well, he did have an exceptional set of teeth, dazzlingly white against the tan. 'It must be brotherly concern, then. But since your good friend looks as if he'd like to put a knife in my back, maybe we should move on. Try a club, maybe?'

Why not? The brunette was clearly intent on getting her wicked way with Robert. Another five minutes and he'd have totally forgotten the bacon sandwich deal, if he hadn't already. Forgotten about her, in all probability until the next time he needed someone to stick a maggot on a hook, or fill in as a date at a dinner party. Well, that was the way she'd chosen to play it, and he did always come back to her for tea and sympathy. If she was careful, he always would.

In the meantime it was rather pleasurable having a good-looking man showing a more than passing interest.

As she looked up at him, it occurred to Daisy that Nick would impress the heck out of her mother. Well, why not? 'Do you have anything planned for two weeks today?' she asked.

Nick opened his mouth, closed it again, then said, 'Not that I can think of.' He flashed his teeth at her again, using them in much the same way as the brunette was using her eyelashes. It could get boring, she decided. 'What do you have in mind?'

'Nothing exciting. I wondered if you'd like to come to my brother's wedding, that's all.'

'Brother as in brother?' He glanced across at Robert. 'Or brother as in ''good friend''?'

'My brother Michael is the one getting married. Robert is just the best man.'

'Then I'm sorry, because I'd love to have come. There's nothing I enjoy more than a good wedding. Unfortunately, I'll be in Perth.'

She considered the logistics of getting him from Scotland... Then the penny dropped. 'You mean Perth, Australia, don't you?'

He was grinning again. She was beginning to suspect he advertised toothpaste for a living. 'I'm afraid I do. But we could still have that date. Give your brother's wedding a miss and come with me. We could have a wedding of our own.' On the other hand there was nothing boring about a man who issued that kind of invitation. Eccentric, perhaps. Over-endowed with imagination, maybe. Drunk, even. Although he didn't sound drunk.

'Well, that's different. But I'm afraid I'll have to say no. I'm fourth bridesmaid, you see.' Although the fact that her mother would never speak to her again if she jetted off to the other side of the world with a complete stranger simply to avoid being fourth bridesmaid might be considered a positive reason for accepting his invitation.

Of course, if she ran away to get married she might just be forgiven. It would certainly put her out of reach of temptation where Robert was concerned. No comfortable back-sliding into gap-filling if she was in Australia. Unfortunately, Nick and his teeth were part of the package.

'They won't miss one bridesmaid, will they?' he pressed, when she didn't immediately answer.

'I'm afraid they would. Three would look so untidy on the photographs. Besides, I make it a rule never to accept proposals of marriage from men I've only just met.'

He wasn't deterred. 'We've got three days before I leave. Plenty of time to get to know one another. Why don't we start with a dance?'

'Three whole days?' she repeated as he relieved her of her glass in a masterful manner and, taking her firmly about the waist, pulled her close. He was more heavily muscled than Robert. Undoubtedly the consequence of hours spent on a surfboard getting that improbable tan. 'You don't waste much time, do you?'

'Life's for living, not wasting.'
he had a point, but she laughed anyway. 'You're crazy.'

He looked hurt. 'Why? Because I want to

get to know you really well? Suppose we were made for each other and you went to this wedding and I went back to Oz and we never found out?'

'That's a risk I'll just have to take,' she said, although she didn't think it was that big a risk. She had the strongest suspicion that he meant getting to 'know' her in the physical sense, rather than intellectually. In fact she suspected that the frank, open, bighearted act was just that. An act. He was just looking for a girl to fill the gap between now and catching his plane, and he wasn't particularly fussy about which girl.

Okay, so she didn't object to filling Robert's little gaps. But she loved Robert. Well. Maybe not right at this moment. At this moment she felt like telling him that he was crazy, too. That life was a two-way street and that if he wasn't careful he'd end up old and lonely. Of course she'd just be wasting her breath. And who was she to tell him that he'd end up old and lonely, when it was far more likely that she'd be the one who was everyone's universal great-aunt rather than anyone's grandmother?

He'd probably still be pulling all the best-looking nurses when he was in his dotage, and she'd probably be the sap pushing his Bath chair.

'Wouldn't you like to find out?' Nick asked, as he came to halt in a corner.

She hadn't been paying too much attention to what he was saying, but this seemed to require an answer. She looked up. 'Find out what?'

Stupid question. The lights were dim, they were in one of those little out of the way corners, and he needed no further invitation to lower his mouth to hers and kiss her.

It was pleasant as kisses went. Nothing heavy. Just a testing-the-water kind of kiss, and Daisy pulled back before it got too serious, looking up at the big, bronzed hunk with just a touch of regret. Her mother would have really loved Nick.

'I'm sorry,' she said. 'I think I'd rather just leave it like this. With you wondering.' She already knew. Had known since her cradle that there was only one man in the world for her.

For a moment Nick looked puzzled. Then he laughed. 'I think I like you.'

'You see? Right decision. Will you excuse me?' She eased herself out of his arms, turned, only to be confronted by Robert.

'You haven't forgotten our deal, have you?' he said, glaring past her at Nick.

Deal? He was still planning on taking her home? 'Oh, for goodness' sake, Robert, go away and flirt with someone your own age,' she said crossly.

'Later. Let's dance.' He didn't wait for an answer, but slipped his arm about her waist. Not like Nick. There had been nothing subtle about the way Nick had held her. He'd held her close, leaving her in no doubt what he was thinking. Robert, of course, didn't see her that way. Usually by this time he'd forgotten all about her. Was he really so upset about Janine's desertion, or was the party lacking in the kind of girls that caught his fancy? 'I'd ask if you were having a good time, but the question would appear to be redundant.'

'It's been interesting,' she said, as they moved together in time to the music. Her cheek was against the peachy twill of his shirt and she could feel the slow thudding of his heartbeat. He didn't dance with her often enough for her to get used to it. Each time was special. The chance to touch him, hold him, feel the hard muscle and bone of his shoulder beneath her hand, breathe in the scent of him, warm and faintly musky. His arm tightened about her possessively and for a long blissful moment she allowed herself to drown in the pleasure of their closeness. Then, because breaking away was so very hard, she added, 'I've already had one proposal of marriage.'

It had the desired effect. He stopped, pulled back a little, his forehead creased in a frown. 'No, I mean really. You seem a bit edgy. Not quite your usual self. You would tell me...'

'What?'

There was a long pause before he said, 'Well, if things weren't...all right.'

'All right?' Of course things weren't all right. He wasn't supposed to take it for granted that she was joking about the proposal, for a start. Okay, so she was, but, really, he might try and play along. 'Well, I may have broken his heart,' she said, 'but I'm sure he'll recover.'

'What?' He frowned. 'What on earth are you talking about?'

'He lives in Australia, you see. If I went to Australia I couldn't be Ginny's bridesmaid. Could I?'

'Er, no, I suppose not.' He seemed be-

mused and Daisy sighed. 'I'm fine, Robert.'
She gave him a little push. 'Go. You've done
your duty. I'm going to see if Monty needs
a hand with the food.' She headed for the
kitchen. Robert followed her, stopping in the
doorway as their host greeted her with
delight.

'Daisy, my darling! Just the girl,' he said,
handing her an apron. 'The caterer left boxes
and boxes of stuff but I haven't got a clue
what to do with it.'

'Stuff that lot in the oven to heat up and
put those on plates. Of course it would save
time, effort and washing up if you just lined
the boxes up on the table. I don't suppose
anyone would notice.'

She saw Robert and Monty exchange a
startled look, and without another word she
tied the apron around her waist, but it occurred to her that she would be better occupied getting to know Nick Gregson, trying to
forget about Robert, than acting as unpaid
kitchen hand. Probably.

She shrugged and gave her attention to the
task in hand, arranging a pile of little savoury
tarts on one plate, heaping chicken goujons
around a bowl of sauce on another. When she

turned to put them on the table, Robert was still standing in the doorway.

It was disconcerting to be the focus of his attention. He didn't usually take so much notice of her, and she couldn't believe that the silver and black top she was wearing was so spectacular that he was unable to take his eyes off her.

'There's another apron if you want to help,' she said.

It had the desired effect. Robert helped himself to a pastry and deserted without another word.

A couple of hours later she'd had enough. She'd passed around food, caught up with the gossip, danced rather more than usual. It was a lovely party, except that every time she turned around Robert seemed to be there, watching her. It was unsettling. She didn't want him looking at her. Not with that little crease that might just be concern dividing his brows. She'd thought she knew everything there was to know about the way his mind worked, but this was different.

Not that things had changed that much. He was still the focus of attention for every unattached girl at the party, and quite a few who weren't, and she had no expectation that, come the witching hour, he would still be looking for a cup of coffee and a bacon sandwich. But there was no way she was going to allow him to delegate the task of seeing her home to anyone else.

Taking advantage of a distraction caused by the still hopeful brunette, she retrieved her coat and considered looking for Monty, but decided instead to phone him later in the week. Nick cut her off before she reached the door.

'Hey! You weren't thinking of leaving without me, were you? We're almost engaged.'

Torn between irritation and a certain satisfaction that someone was capable of seeing more to her than a girl who could fill the gaps, or pass around the canapés, she found herself laughing. 'No, we're not.'

'You're playing very hard to get.' He made it sound as if she was the one being unreasonable.

'I'd hoped you realised I was playing impossible.'

'Nothing is impossible. Once, in Las Vegas, I married a woman I'd only just met.'

'Really?' Why didn't that surprise her? 'Only once?'

'Well—'

'And are you still married to her?'

'Of course not.' He looked hurt at the suggestion. 'I'm not a bigamist. That's the great thing about Las Vegas. Married today...' he clicked his fingers '...divorced tomorrow.'

'Just like that?'

'Well, very nearly.' She wasn't sure whether to believe him or not. On balance she was rather afraid he was telling the truth. 'Where would you like to get married? We could stop over somewhere exotic and have one of those beach ceremonies. I've always rather fancied one of those. What about Bali?'

It was a tough choice. Right now Bali sounded a lot more fun than yellow velvet, but it wasn't really any contest. The dress, after all, was just for a few hours whereas, unlike Nick, she viewed marriage as a lifetime commitment. 'I'm allergic to sand,' she said. 'And I'm scared of flying.'

'Are you?' That seemed to throw him momentarily. 'A shipboard wedding, then? The ship's captain doing the honours?'

'It's a myth that you can be legally married by the captain of a ship,' she told him. The joke was beginning to wear very thin.

'And right now all I'm interested in is going home. Alone.' She turned and walked out into the street.

He wasn't that easy to shake off. 'The streets aren't safe for a woman on her own,' he said, following her.

'Maybe not, but how safe are they with you?'

And this time when he smiled she fancied it was less a sexual display of teeth than genuine good humour. 'As safe as you want them to be. Scout's honour,' he promised.

Before she could tell him that she didn't believe he had ever been a Scout, he had hailed a passing black cab.

'Daisy!' *Robert*. 'There you are, sweetheart. I was looking for you. I'm just about ready for the coffee and sandwich you promised,' he said, taking her arm and smiling cordially at Nick as he opened the taxi door and held it for her while she stepped inside. 'Thanks for the taxi, Gregson. Black cabs are as rare as hen's teeth at this time of night.'

And with that he stepped in after her and closed the door, leaving Nick Gregson standing alone on the pavement as they drove away.

CHAPTER THREE

SUNDAY 26 March. Church with family for final reading of the Banns for Michael and Ginny's wedding and everyone home for lunch afterwards. Mother will be in her element.

Robert offered me a lift. I said I'd rather walk. I do hope he didn't take me seriously.

'Daisy?'

She knew it was him as soon as the doorbell rang. Even at the crack of dawn her heart gave one of those painful leaps that betrayed her every time.

She glanced at her watch, yawned, tightened the belt of her dressing gown about her waist. Why was it so much harder to get up in London than in the country? 'Go away, Robert. It's the middle of the night.'

'It's seven-thirty. Halfway through the day.'

'Is it?' She blinked at her watch. 'Oh,

Lord, so it is. I thought it said twenty-five to six.'

'Perhaps you'd better get some spectacles.'

'I don't need spectacles; I need more sleep. Did you have to come this early?'

'No, but I was rather hoping you'd make me some breakfast. Since I didn't get the supper you promised.'

'You didn't deserve supper.'

'Maybe not. But then I never said I was perfect.' No. He'd never said that. 'Pretty damn near, though.' She could hear the smile in his voice and she rested her forehead against the door. Yes. Pretty damn near.

'You don't deserve breakfast, either.'

'No? Who else would get up at the crack of dawn to give an ungrateful brat a lift home?'

'You were going home anyway.' She released the door catch. 'But I suppose you'd better come up,' she said, and retreated to the kitchen to make coffee. She heard him come in, knew the very moment he came to a halt in the doorway behind her.

'You're not really angry with me.' It wasn't a question. He said it with the confidence of a man who knew he was irresistible.

She didn't turn around; she knew he would be smiling and of course his smile *would be* totally irresistible.

It wasn't fair. But then who said life had to be fair? If it was fair she'd have the same sleek hair as her sister, the same lovely figure, or, failing that, at least Michael's height. But her siblings had inherited all the most attractive genes from both parents and there hadn't been any left over for her.

'Of course I'm angry with you,' she replied, keeping her back firmly to him. 'Just because you've been abandoned by man's best reason to stay in bed on a Sunday morning, there's no need to wake me up at the crack of dawn.'

'I meant about last night.'

'Last night?' She pretended to think. 'Oh, you mean about Nick? Thanks for reminding me. For once in my life I managed to bag the best-looking man at the party...' he snorted derisively '...and you chased him off in case you missed out on your supper.'

'I missed out anyway,' he pointed out.

She spun around. 'You didn't think I was going to feed you after that?'

'I was simply taking care of you. Did you know he's divorced? Gregson,' he added, in case she wasn't sure. 'Twice. Monty told me.'

'Monty's an old gossip.'

'He's the diary editor of a national newspaper. Gossip is what he does.'

Daisy shrugged. Twice? It figured. A man that quick with his proposals was bound to get caught out once in a while. 'You didn't think I'd be tempted to become wife number three, did you?'

'Well—'

The wretch sounded doubtful. 'Do you imagine I'd contemplate marrying a complete stranger on the spur of the moment? On a whim?' She poured the near boiling water on the coffee.

'It happens. He's got two alimony payments to prove it. And you said it; he is good-looking...if you go for the muscle-bound type.' Robert was leaning against the doorjamb, arms folded, legs crossed, and the casual arrogance of the man suddenly infuriated her.

'It may interest you to know, Robert, that some of us require a little more substance before we fall into bed...' She knew as soon as the words left her tongue that she'd said the wrong thing. His head came up sharply, and although his posture hadn't changed significantly, it was no longer relaxed. 'I realise that he wasn't on your approved list of escorts, that he couldn't be relied upon to report back.' Robert said nothing. She ploughed on nervously. 'Heavens, I might even have been tempted to try him out—on approval, as it were...'

'I imagine that he was the one with that in mind,' he said abruptly.

'What's the matter, Robert? You can play the field but I have to be tucked up safely in my virginal little bed by midnight? Is that it? Sauce for the goose, my friend...'

'I thought we had decided that you were a duck—' She glared at him. He held up his hands in mock surrender. 'You know Michael would have done exactly the same if he'd been there.'

'Michael is my brother. What's your excuse?'

'Good grief, Daisy, I'm beginning to think you were seriously taken in by the man.'

He sounded positively affronted, and Daisy, concentrating on stirring the coffee, allowed a tiny smile of satisfaction to soften her mouth. She might not have welcomed the manner in which he'd taken charge last night, but she was human enough to take some pleasure from the fact that he'd cared enough to abandon the lovely brunette in order to charge to her rescue. 'Quite the contrary. It was the fact that you'd think I might have been taken in by him that made me mad.'

'What? Oh, I see. Well, for that I do apologise.' She kept her back to him while she struggled to bring a wild urge to grin firmly under control. She simply allowed her shoulders to lift an inch or two in an unimpressed shrug. 'Sincerely,' he added. She picked a couple of mugs off the stand. 'Am I forgiven?'

'This time,' she conceded, with every appearance of reluctance. Duck, indeed.

'I am sorry, you know. About last night. I'm afraid I take you for granted.'

She finally turned, solemnly meeting his honey-brown gaze. 'Yes, Robert, you do. But only because I allow you to.' And the room seethed with silence as Robert digested her remark. 'So, what did you have in mind for breakfast?' she asked brightly, to break the sudden tension.

For a moment he remained quite still, a frown marking the space between his eyes.

Then he turned away and opened the fridge door. 'It would be a pity to let that bacon go to waste,' he said, scanning the contents. 'Except that you don't appear to have any bacon.'

'No.'

'You never intended to feed me last night, did you?'

'I never imagined I would have to. Scrambled eggs?' she offered, reaching past him and taking a box of eggs from the fridge without waiting for an answer.

'Daisy...'

She cracked the eggs carefully into a basin. 'Get some plates out of that cupboard, will you?' she asked, as she began to beat them.

He found the plates, set a couple of places at her kitchen table. 'Daisy, can I ask you something?'

'Will you put some bread in the toaster?' she countered. She had the feeling he was going to ask her what she was doing when he wasn't monopolising her time, taking her for granted. What could she say? That she was busy improving her knowledge of oriental pottery? That she read a lot? Spent far too much time watching stupid television programmes? All true. Not that she didn't have a social life. Far from it. But not the kind of social life that Robert had suddenly developed an interest in. It was a conversation she had always sought to avoid, but, suddenly ambushed, she had every intention of fighting a spirited rearguard action. 'It's over there,' she prompted, when he didn't move. 'In the breadbin.'

'Right.' He finally took the hint and did as she asked. She glanced up from the eggs, suspicious of such an easy victory.

Daisy left Robert to deal with the dishes, while she showered, battened down her still damp hair in a French plait and dressed in an undemanding grey skirt that wouldn't crumple in the car. She stuffed a pair of jeans and a sweatshirt in a small bag, along with a pair of boots so that she could take the dog for a walk after lunch, and some calming bathtime treats she'd bought for her mother. The role of groom's mother might not be quite as stressful as that of mother of the bride, but she had a feeling they would still be needed. Maybe she should lay in a stock for her own use.

'Ready?'

Robert had made fresh coffee and helped himself to her newspaper. 'I've been ready for half an hour,' he said, folding the paper and getting to his feet.

'And it's still not nine o'clock.' She tutted, shaking her head. 'You'd better get yourself another girl and quick, or Sundays are going to seem very long.'

'I do have other interests, you know.' She gave him the kind of look that suggested she wasn't fooled for a minute. He grinned. 'It's true. I like to fish.'

'And when was the last time you went fishing?'

'I don't know.' He thought about it as they walked down the stairs. 'A couple of weeks ago?' he offered. 'You were with me.'

'Then it was before Christmas. You met Janine at a Christmas party and I haven't been fishing since...'

'Ouch.'

'So, do you want to hear about the three little maids?'

He frowned. 'Who?'

'The luscious bridesmaids,' she reminded him, as he held the car door for her, saw her settled into the thick leather upholstery and then climbed behind the wheel. 'They were going to draw lots for you, you know.'

'Lots? Do you mean with me as prize?' He sounded shocked. Daisy was not totally convinced by that shock. Any man would be flattered by such attention. 'They wouldn't.'

'Well, no, they didn't.' She allowed a pause for an expression of relief then, when he'd obliged, she continued. 'In the end they decided there was no point.'

'Oh?' Daisy had been a sister all her life and she knew there wasn't a man born who could resist that little querying, 'Oh?'

She smiled demurely. 'It was obvious that none of them trusted the others to play fair.'

He threw her a startled glance. 'You're making this up.'

'I think Diana will be the most...' she searched for the right word '...inventive.'

'You're just having a little fun at my expense—'

As if she would... 'Then there's Maud.'

'Maud? What a sweet, old-fashioned name.' His voice had changed very subtly. She recognised every nuance, knew that he had caught on to the game and was now playing along with her.

'For a sweet old-fashioned girl.' The kind

that believes in marriage. 'She's pretty, Robert. Very pretty. And quietly confident. She knows the hotel where the reception is being held and I fancy she's already worked out where she's going to ambush you. There's a huge, rather gothic conservatory, apparently.'

'That would be the place. I just love gothic conservatories, don't you?' Chance would be a fine thing, Daisy thought. 'And very appropriate for a girl called Maud. And?' She raised a brow in silent query. 'There are three of them. What does number three have in mind?'

Playing the game and already one step ahead. 'If you come through rounds one and two unscathed, Robert, I think I can guarantee that Fiona will ensure that you don't get bored.'

'It's going to be an interesting day. Thanks for the warning. I'll treat you to lunch somewhere quiet on the Sunday after the wedding and tell you how they performed, shall I?'

Quite without warning, the joke turned sour in her mouth. Daisy might have been making up stories to tease him with, but they wouldn't be that far off the mark. She could cope with Robert's 'girls' in theory. At a distance. She didn't want to hear about them. 'Lunch will be lovely, but you can keep the macho stuff for the men's room. I'm far too young for such tales.'

'Probably.' Then he glanced at her. 'Although Nick Gregson didn't seem to think so.'

'Nick Gregson is just an overgrown adolescent. What would he know?'

Robert dropped Daisy at her parents' home, on the opposite side of the village from the house where his mother had lived since she'd divorced his father.

She opened the door quickly, not waiting for him to do it for her and slid out of the seat. 'Thanks, for the lift. See you in church.'

He watched her walk quickly away down the path, then, as she disappeared round side of the house, he eased the big car slowly around the village green, deep in thought.

Just how old was Daisy? He'd known her since she was a baby. She'd always been there, toddling after Michael, toddling after both of them. A real nuisance. Then a real pain of a tomboy. Then a gawky teenager. The braces had long disappeared from her teeth, but she still wore her hair in a plait, or tied back in a band. She still wore jeans and a baggy sweatshirt most of the time. He'd have said she still looked like a teenager, except teenagers made a lot more effort to look twenty. And last night—

'Robert!' His mother met him at the gate. She'd been walking her elderly Labrador and the dog waddled up as fast as middle-aged spread would allow, his entire body wagging from side to side as he swung his heavy tail to show his excitement.

'Hey, steady, Major!' He rubbed the dog's ear, kissed his mother's cheek and walked with her round to the back of the house and into the mud room.

'I didn't expect you so early,' she said, putting some bare larch twigs into the old stone sink before bending to wipe the dog's paws with a piece of towelling.

'I gave Daisy a lift.'

'Did you?' She paused for a moment, then said, 'Well, it's nice to have company. Pass me that jug, will you, darling, and give Major some water?' Robert handed her a big stone jug, then filled the dog's bowl while she arranged the larch. 'I haven't seen Daisy for weeks. How is she?'

'Getting into a bit of a stew about the wedding. You know she's had to stand in for one of the bridesmaids at the last minute?'

'Her mother told me. Margaret's delighted, of course.'

'Margaret might give Daisy's feelings a little consideration. She hates the very idea.'

'Does she? How odd. Most girls would love to dress up and be the centre of attention.'

'Oh, come on. You know Daisy better than that. She never dresses up.' Well, hardly ever. She'd looked pretty special for Monty's party. Or for whoever she'd seen before Monty's party. The idea that there had been someone had lodged in his brain and refused to go away. She might have flirted with Gregson at the party, but she hadn't really been bothered when he'd been left behind on the pavement. No matter how much she'd pretended. He frowned. It wasn't like her to make such a fuss.

'Doesn't she?' His mother turned with the jug and stood it in the windowsill to catch the sun. 'I didn't realise you saw her that often.'

'We have lunch sometimes.' What did she do the rest of the time? She never talked much. She listened brilliantly, though.

Maybe he should take a leaf from her book; he might learn something. 'And I took her to Monty Sheringham's party last night.' He shrugged as his mother glanced at him. 'She was going anyway.'

'I assume that means Janine is history?'

'Her decision. She was looking for a husband, a family. The whole "till death us do part" bit.'

'In other words, all the things you think you're incapable of offering.'

'Happy is the man who knows his limitations.'

'Maybe.' She patted his arm absently. 'Although I sometimes think that whoever said "ignorance is bliss" had a point. I often wish that I'd never found out about your father's amorous adventures. I'd probably still be happily married to him.'

'Living a lie?'

'We all live lies to a greater or lesser degree, darling. You allow the young women who fall in love with you to hope that you might be persuaded to change your mind about marriage.'

'I always make my feelings on the subject absolutely clear.'

'But they don't believe you. And you

know they don't believe you.' She shrugged. 'They simply pretend they aren't interested in marriage while they set about convincing you it is the one thing in the world you need.'

'That's very cynical.'

'But nevertheless true. Why don't you make some coffee while I take a shower?'

'Can I ask you something?' His mother paused at the foot of the stairs. 'You never stopped loving him, did you?'

'Your father? You've seen him recently?' The way her face lit up from the inside was all the answer he needed.

'He called me, wanted to talk, so we had dinner. He asked about you. He always asks about you.'

'He's getting old, and girls aren't quite so thick on the ground these days. How is he?' Robert shrugged and his mother laid an understanding hand upon on his shoulder. 'You're not like him, you know.'

'On the contrary. Seeing him is like looking into a mirror thirty years from now.'

'Looks mean nothing. It's what you are inside that matters. But you're right, of course. I never stopped loving him.'

'So why didn't you just look the other way? Nothing had changed, after all.'

'Now who's being cynical?' Then she shook her head. 'If I could have ignored the facts, darling, I would have. For you as well as for me. But once you're faced with reality, nothing can ever be the same.'

'You've really got to take more of an interest in yourself, Daisy.' Her mother was shaking her head. 'Don't you care what kind of impression you make? You should take a leaf out of your sister's book—'

Sarah and her husband were sitting in state in the living room, ensuring that their exquisitely dressed children didn't get dirty before church.

'We're going to church, Mum, not a fashion parade. Can I give you a hand in the kitchen?'

'Mrs Banks has got everything under control. Come upstairs and I'll see what I can do with your hair.'

Daisy threw a mute, impassioned plea towards her father. David Galbraith shuffled his feet, cleared his throat, glanced at his watch. 'I think I'll, er, go and talk to Andrew.' His wife waved him away impatiently as she ushered Daisy upstairs and then circled her like a hungry shark.

Twenty minutes later Margaret Galbraith admitted defeat and allowed Daisy to weave her hair back into a French plait. 'It's all your father's fault, of course.'

'What is?'

'All his family have impossible hair,' her mother replied obliquely. 'Michael and Sarah take after me, thankfully, but you...' She sighed. 'You're going to have to do something about it before the wedding.'

'Yes, Mother,' she said meekly. Her mother gave her a sharp look. 'I am,' she protested. 'Ginny gave me the number of her hairdresser. He's coming down to do everyone's hair on the day, but he wants to see me first so that he'll know what he's faced with. I've an appointment at the crack of dawn on Monday.'

'Oh, well, that's something, I suppose.' Margaret Galbraith didn't sound entirely convinced. Flicking a dissatisfied eye over her daughter and the simple grey skirt she was wearing, she said, 'It's not too late to change, you know. That skirt is so dull and so long. Now, I've got a gorgeous little pink two-piece which would be absolutely perfect—'

Pink! Yellow! All it would take was a

scoop of nuts and a dollop of chocolate sauce and she'd turn into an ice cream sundae. 'You've got me into a bridesmaid's frock, Mother. Can we leave it at that for now? Please?'

Her mother struggled to hold her tongue for a moment before giving a little couldn't-care-less shrug. 'What are they like? The bridesmaids' dresses?'

'They are *so-o-o* pretty.' Daisy gushed with enthusiasm. Anything to change the subject. And they *were* pretty. If you were a buxom brunette. Maybe she *should* get a lift 'em up and push 'em together bra as recommended by Robert. Presumably he knew what he was talking about. It might help, and she wouldn't, after all, be competing with the other girls. She didn't have their natural advantages, for one thing. But she would be able to look her mother in the eye and say she'd tried, without having to cross her fingers behind her back.

Her mother was temporarily distracted by her description of the dresses, then Michael arrived and she hurried downstairs, forgetting all about Daisy.

'Hi, sis.' Michael gave her a hug and a slightly sardonic smile, once he'd extricated himself from his mother. 'Thanks for stepping into the breach.' She could see by his face that he knew what an effort it must be.

'Hey. No problem. Where's Ginny?'

'I dropped her off at home. She's walking over to church with her parents.' He grinned. 'All very proper. What about you? All alone?'

'Well, I did pick up this really gorgeous man at a party last night. A big suntanned Australian. Mum would have loved him, but unfortunately Robert disapproved and saw him off.' Michael's brows lifted in surprise. 'Apparently he'd been married a couple of times already.'

'Oh, I see. Well, Robert's always been very protective where you're concerned.'

'Has he?' Daisy's cheeks heated up. That wouldn't do. She had the feeling that Michael was the one person in the entire world who suspected how she felt about Robert. 'Yes, well, he doesn't have a little sister to boss about, does he?' she said, just a touch sharply. 'And you've always shared everything with him.'

Michael's grin widened. 'Not quite everything. If he wants a wife he's going to have to find one of his own.'

'He doesn't. Want a wife.'

'He just says that. He hasn't met the right woman, that's all.'

'I *see*. That's his excuse for going through so many of them.' Michael laughed and Daisy made a pretty good fist of joining in. It was only the cast-iron belief that Robert was in deadly earnest about not getting married that made his romantic entanglements bearable. The knowledge that he would always be there.

But suddenly a moment of doubt assailed her, catching at her breath. What if Michael was right? What if, one day, Robert turned up with a wife on his arm? Because that was how it would happen. He wouldn't submit to all this performance. He'd simply disappear to the Caribbean, or the Pacific, or somewhere...

'It's time we were leaving,' Margaret Galbraith said, emerging from the kitchen, smoothing on her gloves. 'Daisy? Are you wearing a hat?'

'What? Oh, no.'

'That's a pity. There's nothing like a hat for disguising problem hair. I'll find you something—'

Daisy snapped out of her distraction,

caught Michael's eye and, dredging up a big smile from somewhere, linked her arm through his and headed for the front gate before her mother had a chance to dig out some awful felt monstrosity and insist she wear it.

'Come on, Michael Galbraith, bachelor of this parish. This is it, for the last time of asking. Time's running out.'

'It can't run out fast enough for me. Just wait, you'll see.'

'Me? No way. I'm with Robert on this one...'

'Daisy!' She turned at the sound of Jennifer Furneval's voice and, surrendering Michael's arm as he joined Robert, she walked across the green towards the older woman, who kissed her cheek and fell in beside her as they walked towards the church. 'I'm so glad to see you.'

'How are you, Jennifer?'

'Well enough. Robert said he gave you a lift down this morning. You don't have a car of your own?'

'I don't see the point in London. Although if I'm going to be travelling to auctions I'll have to think about it.'

'George has surrendered that chore to you, has he?'

'Well, maybe. I'm going to a country house sale in the Wye Valley next week.' She mentioned the location. 'There's an interesting collection of oriental pieces being auctioned. Maybe you're going?'

'Unfortunately I can't. There is a piece of Imari ware I particularly like the look of, but it's too risky putting in a phone bid for something on the evidence of a photograph.'

'I could check it out and phone you. If you trust my judgement. And I'll be happy to bid for you, too. I understand I owe you a big thank-you for my job.'

Jennifer laughed. 'Nonsense. I was doing George the favour. How is he?'

'Another one bites the dust, eh, Rob? Although rumour has it that this time the lady jumped before she was pushed.'

'Janine?' Robert shrugged, hiding his increasing irritation that no one seemed surprised by the break-up, just vaguely amused that this time he was the one who'd been dumped. 'It was inevitable. She's a peach, but getting to that time of life when the biological clock is demanding a mortgage and babies with increasing persistence.'

Michael grinned. 'So?'

'So, my biological clock is on a go-slow. Or maybe it never got wound up. Michael, I'm a bit concerned about Daisy,' he said, changing the subject. He had more on his mind than a girl who was already history.

'Daisy? Why? What's she been doing?'

'I'm not sure. She never talks much about herself, did you notice that? Most girls are bubbling over with who they're seeing, where they've been.' He glanced ahead. She was chatting away to his mother easily enough, but that would be about their shared passion for porcelain. 'Has she always been secretive, or is it a new thing?'

'You see as much of her as I do.' They had fallen behind the others and Michael came to halt. 'But, yes, she is very...private. So what's bothering you?'

If he knew that, he wouldn't be bothered; he'd be dealing with it. 'Nothing I can put my finger on exactly. But last night I took her to Monty Sheringham's party. I thought we'd have dinner first, but she said she was busy until ten. She said she was working.'

'But you didn't believe her?'

'She didn't look as if she'd been working. She looked...fired up, different. I just got this feeling that there was a man involved. Mike, do you think she could be having an affair?'

'An affair? What a wonderfully old-fashioned word.' Then, as he caught on, 'With a married man, you mean? Daisy?' And he laughed. 'Are you crazy?'

'I know it seems unlikely, but what else could it be? If it was straightforward she'd have brought him to the party, or gone somewhere else with him—'

'Rob...' Michael interrupted him as if he knew something, was about to tell him something.

'What?' But Daisy's brother simply shook his head and walked on. 'You know something, don't you?' Robert wanted to grab him by the throat and throttle it out of him. 'Tell me...' He realised that Michael was staring at him and he turned away, stuffed his hands hard into his pockets and resumed walking towards the church. 'I'm sorry. But she's always been there for me, Mike. I don't want to see her making the kind of mistake that will ruin her life.'

'I don't think she has much of a choice about that,' Michael said, falling in beside him. 'You're right, of course. There's a man she's been in love with for a very long time, but marriage appears to be out of the question.'

'In love?' He hadn't taken his eyes off her, and now she was standing at the lych gate of the church in a little knot of people, laughing at something his mother had said to her. The early spring sunshine was lighting up the tiny wisps of hair that had escaped from her plait like a halo, and as the sound of her laughter reached him he felt a sharp stab of envy for the man who could capture her heart and hold it. 'Who is he?'

'I really don't think she'd want me to tell you that.'

'Why? What's the big secret?' He turned back to Michael. 'I was right. He's married, isn't he?'

'Look, forget it, will you? I shouldn't have said anything.' Mike was plainly uncomfortable about something. 'Daisy is old enough to make her own decisions.' Then he shrugged. 'Whether they're the right ones...'

'He's married but he can't possibly leave his wife.' Robert knew the type. He'd be the kind of man who would invent some tale about his wife being chronically ill, or hooked on tranquillisers, or alcohol, or anything that meant it was impossible for him to leave the children. He'd manage to appear vulnerable and hurting and at the same time incredibly noble: a lethal combination, particularly when the girl was young and vulnerable herself. And, of course, any woman who got involved with him would understand from the outset that divorce was utterly impossible. 'I knew there was someone on Saturday night—'

Michael grasped the opportunity to change the subject. 'A big Australian, so Daisy told me,' he said, laughing. 'She was hoping to bring him along to the wedding to distract Mum. You are not in her good books.'

He couldn't believe Michael could be so blasé about this, and he refused to be distracted by a twice-married Australian. 'I can't believe you're taking this so lightly! She's your sister, for heaven's sake. You've got to do something...'

'She doesn't need me to wet nurse her. Daisy knows what she's doing.' Michael glanced at him. 'She always has.'

'How can you say that? She's a child and she's going to get hurt.'

'Actually, Rob, she's a grown woman. She's twenty-four,' he added, just to make his point.

'Twenty-four?' But she was just a baby—'

'When you were seven years old. You'll be thirty next birthday. We both will.'

'Twenty-four?' He stopped. 'Good lord. I always think of her as your kid sister.' Or he had, until Saturday. *Twenty-four? Where had the years gone?* He turned to Michael. 'She is *still* your kid sister, Mike, even if she is twenty-four. Have you talked to her about this?'

'No. We've never talked about it. And she'd be devastated if she knew I'd mentioned it to you.'

'Would she? Why?'

'Trust me, Robert. I know what I'm talking about.' Michael gave him a sideways look. 'You won't say anything to her? It's your duty as best man to get me to the altar in one piece,' Mike prompted in the face of his hesitation.

'I won't say a word.' And he wouldn't, although he was oddly hurt that she hadn't confided in him. He told her everything. 'I'm not promising I won't do something, though.'

'Oh? What have you got in mind?'

'Find out who he is and tell him to take a hike. Any objections?'

Michael shook his head and Robert could have sworn he was doing his best not to smile. 'None whatever, Galahad. In fact I'd be most interested to know how you get on.'

'It isn't funny, Mike.' Daisy was his friend, the one person who was always there when he needed her, quick with a kind word, quicker still with a sharp one when he was in danger of pomposity. More than that, she was a girl who was not afraid of silence.

He always felt *renewed* by her company, and he was damned if he was going to stand by and let some selfish lout break her heart.

CHAPTER FOUR

SUNDAY 26 March. I've never seen Michael so happy. He arrived at church with such a ridiculous I-know-something-nobody-else-knows smirk on his face that really it almost made me want to slap him. Anyone would think he was the first man in the world to fall in love. If just reading the last of the Banns makes him feel that good, heaven knows what the wedding will do to him. Ginny is so lucky.

Robert, on the other hand, is acting very oddly. Almost as if he can't bear to let me out of his sight. Weird.

'What time do you want to leave?' Daisy asked.

Michael and Ginny had made a move soon after lunch and everyone else had quickly followed. But Robert appeared to be in no hurry to get back to London. His mother had been invited to lunch, but had other plans, and now he was stretched out languidly in front of the fire, chatting to her father. 'There's no rush.' Then his look became more intent. 'Is there?'

'No. I just wondered if I had time to take Flossie for a run, get a blow of fresh air before we drive back.' Her mother's spaniel lifted her head at the sound of her name and Daisy, who had changed into the comfort of jeans the minute they had returned from church, slapped her thigh encouragingly. 'I'll make some tea when I get back.'

'Wait. I'll come with you.'

'You don't have to—' she began, ignoring the sudden charge of her heart at the prospect. She tried not to appear too eager for his company. It wasn't always easy.

'On the contrary,' he interrupted, before she could finish making her point that he wasn't exactly dressed for a muddy lane. It was hard, wanting something with all your heart that you knew you could never have. Walks with Robert were bliss, and she craved them, but she knew she would pay for self-indulgence with long hours when the loneliness would seem all the more intense. 'I definitely need to walk off the effects of your mother's cooking.' Daisy raised her eyebrows in disbelief as he got to his feet.

Square at the shoulders, slender at the hips and with not an ounce of spare fat anywhere in between, the idea of Robert needing exercise to keep in trim was laughable. He caught her look and shrugged. 'You don't think I keep this way overdoing it on the apple pie, do you? Pastry like that has to paid for with pain.'

'Oh, well, just as long as walking with me is a penance for gluttony, you're very welcome. You can borrow a pair of Dad's wellingtons,' she said, with all the carelessness she could muster. It was getting harder. Maybe it was the wedding, Ginny and Michael's obvious happiness, the knowledge that she wouldn't ever have that, because marriage to anyone else would be settling for second best. Never an option.

Margaret Galbraith put her head around the door. 'Is anyone ready for tea? Oh, are you leaving already?'

'No, Mum. Just taking Flossie for a run. Put your feet up and I'll see to the tea when we get back. Robert will help me.'

'Will I?' he asked, surprised.

'You've got to burn off those calories, remember?'

'Well, I must say that would be pleasant,'

Margaret Galbraith said, subsiding onto the sofa. 'You won't go far, will you? It looks as if it might rain any minute.'

'I'll look after her, Margaret.' Robert's hand on her shoulder was unexpected and she jumped. 'Come on, Flossie,' he said. 'Walkies.' Flossie needed no second bidding. Some things could be relied upon never to change.

They walked in silence for a while, following the lane down to the river, Flossie bounding ahead of them, starting up a pheasant. 'Are you still mad at me for cutting out Nick Gregson?' he asked, after a while.

'Don't be silly.'

'Am I? Being silly? You've avoided me all day.'

'I've been busy all day. And, if you must know, I only flirted with Nick because I hoped he might come to the wedding. As my date. Unfortunately he's going back to Oz on Tuesday.'

'Three days is a long time in a relationship.'

'It didn't take three hours to work out that Nick wasn't exactly my cup of tea, but that's the trouble with asking men out. They think you fancy them.'

'Equality has downs as well as ups.' He stopped on the path and she turned, sure he was laughing at her, but when she looked up his face, shadowed in the gathering gloom of the threatening rain, was still, intense. 'Would I do? As a date?'

Her heart leapt, her pulse quickened and all those other stupid things that could get a girl into all kinds of trouble. 'No, Robert. You wouldn't do at all. My mother wouldn't take you seriously.'

'Your mother!' He laughed. Then he wasn't laughing. 'Oh, I see. Your mother.'

'Exactly. I could never convince her that you were likely husband material, could I?'

He didn't answer and they walked on for a while, the silence more oppressive, full of the unspoken, the unspeakable.

'I was thinking,' Robert said finally. 'There's no reason why we couldn't stay overnight and drive back first thing in the morning. We could take a stroll down to the pub later.'

A stroll down to the village pub, the chance to spend an hour beside the fire, just the two of them. She'd had Robert's undivided attention all day and now this. It was too much. It was perhaps just as well that she was unable to succumb to temptation. 'I'm sorry, Robert, but I do have to be back tonight.'

'Oh, well. Just a thought. Are you going somewhere later?'

Daisy glanced at him. He wasn't usually that interested in what she was doing. But he was looking straight ahead and she couldn't see what he was thinking. 'No, I've got a particularly early start in the morning, that's all.'

'I wouldn't have put George Latimer down as a slave-driver, but first he has you working on Saturday evening and now he wants you in at the crack of dawn on Monday. Perhaps I should have a word with him on the subject of employment law.'

'No,' she said, quickly. 'It isn't work.' The last thing she wanted was Robert quizzing George about Saturday. 'I'm going to see the wedding hairdresser. Eight o'clock tomorrow morning was the only time we could both manage this week. I've got the final fitting for the bridesmaid dress, too. No lunch for me, either.'

'I see.' He glanced down at her, smiling a little. 'You're going to have your feathers clipped, are you?'

'Lord knows. He's going to try and sort out some way to make my hair and the head-dress compatible. Poor man, no one should be put through that first thing on a Monday morning.'

'Your hair looked very pretty on Saturday night. You should wear it loose more often.'

Daisy managed to retrieve her mouth before it hit the ground, and since Flossie chose that precise moment to chase a duck into a thicket, she used the excuse to dive after them both, thus avoiding the need to say anything.

By the time she had caught the dog, extricated her from the thicket and made sure that the duck was unharmed, her hair had been largely wrenched from its plait and was anything but pretty. But at least the need to comment upon the unexpected compliment had passed.

She was always doing that, Robert realised, as she fidgeted with escaping wisps of hair. Mocking her appearance before someone else could do it for her. A habit she had slipped into, he had no doubt, to protect herself from her mother's incessant comparison with her older sister. He'd never been able to see it. Sarah might be attractive in a conventional, exquisitely groomed sort of way, but she talked too much and, unlike Daisy, she rarely listened.

But maybe it was like a dripping tap; if someone constantly undermined your self-confidence you might, eventually, begin to believe them.

Was that what was behind her secret affair? He had always thought of Daisy as a strong person, but everyone had their weaknesses. If some man without morals or principles had latched onto that insecurity, she might have been vulnerable.

'You don't mind going back this evening, do you?' she asked, after a while.

'No. Not at all.' Did she really have an early start, he wondered, or was she hoping to snatch an hour with the mysterious lover? 'It was just that today reminded me what we've been missing.' He came to halt when they reached the towpath. 'It seems to me that all my best days were spent on this riverbank. Do you remember that time Mike poked a stick in a wasps' nest and they flew into your hair?'

'Oh, yes, that was a *lot* of fun. Especially

the bit where you threw me into the river so I wouldn't get stung.'

'I pulled you out.'

'Yes, Robert, you pulled me out. And you picked the soggy wasps out of my hair and you were the one who got stung.' She lifted his hand and held it between her own. 'Your fingers were so swollen and red.' She turned it over, rubbed her thumb over the scar along his knuckles. 'And you got this when you dragged Billy Pemberton's dog off me.' She looked up. 'I was a bit of nuisance, wasn't I?'

'A total pain,' he agreed. 'We only put up with you because you always had the sense to bring food.'

'I knew you wouldn't send me home if I brought sandwiches.'

Six years old and she'd already known the way to a man's heart, he thought. 'Maybe we should come down next weekend. If you bring the food, I'll bring the maggots.' She didn't leap at the idea. 'If you're not working late again.'

'I'm not sure. It's going to be a bit hectic this week. I'm going away for a couple of days on a buying trip. Can I let you know?'

'Do that. I'll give you my mobile number,

just in case I'm not in the office.' They walked on for a while. 'Where are you going? On this buying trip?'

'It's a country house sale,' she said, apparently glad to change the subject. 'In the Wye Valley. I may be bidding for something for your mother, too. There's an Imari bowl she'd like, but she can't get to the sale herself.'

'Really?' He'd never given much thought to what she did at the gallery. His mother had told him that Latimer needed a dogsbody and she'd thought Daisy would enjoy working for him. And, from the way Daisy talked about her job, he had assumed she spent her days answering the telephone, making the tea and dusting the treasures. Apparently it was not just her mother who underestimated her. 'That sounds like fun.'

'I'm a bit nervous to tell you truth. It's the first time George has allowed me out with the chequebook on my own.'

She gave a little shiver. Nerves, he thought, rather than the temperature, but he stuck his hands in his pockets and poked out his elbow, offering her his arm. 'Here, tuck in, keep warm.' After the slightest hesitation she did as he said, looping her arm through his. How long had that hesitation been there? Since she'd had this mysterious lover? The thought of her lying in the arms of some unknown man made his guts twist uncomfortably, and he tucked her arm hard against his side, wanting to hold her, keep her safe.

She shivered again. 'I think it's time we went back,' she said. 'Flossie! Here, girl!' And before he could stop her she had extricated her arm from his. 'Race you!' she said, and set off back down the path. 'Last one back cleans the dog.' From behind, she still looked like the lean-limbed girl he remembered. But his mother was right. Once you'd seen the reality, you recognised the deception. Daisy Galbraith might wear her hair in a plait, but, whatever else she was, she certainly wasn't Michael's kid sister any more.

It was nearly eight by the time they arrived back at Daisy's apartment. 'Thanks for the lift today, Robert. I really appreciated it,' she said, not waiting for him to open the car door for her but bounding out, as if she couldn't wait to get rid of him.

He ignored the unspoken suggestion that she didn't want company. Every time he'd edged the conversation in her direction on the way home, attempting to discover what she'd been doing, who she'd been seeing, she'd diverted his interest by regaling him with the wonders of her new computer. Well, two could play at that game. 'Grateful enough to let me have a look at this fabulous PC of yours?'

She looked at him as if he were crazy. 'Don't you see enough of them at the bank?'

'It's not the same. My mother was talking about getting one, hooking up to the internet, getting into e-mail; with her worldwide contacts, it makes sense. Since you're so enthusiastic about yours, I thought maybe it would suit her. Is it easy to use?'

'Piece of cake. I'll send you the details.'

'Show me.' He locked the car door, ignoring all the "go away" signals. 'Of course, I wouldn't say no to a cup of cocoa,' he added. 'If you're making one.' Well, it was exactly the sort of thing she would expect him to say. 'In fact I wouldn't say no to a piece of cake, either. Real, rather than virtual.'

'I don't do cake.'

'Toast will do.'

'All right,' she said, relenting. 'You can come up for half an hour. Not a minute longer. I'm planning on an early night. I need all the beauty sleep I can get.'

'Whatever you say,' he replied, because that was what he always said.

'My hero,' she said wryly, and then laughed. She was a lot more comfortable with his casual insults than with his earlier comment about her hair, he noticed. She didn't want his compliments. Well, she wasn't exactly used to getting them. Why? Compliments were second nature to him.

'I make it a rule never to disagree with a lady,' he said easily, but it occurred to him that her skin was flawless and her hair might be unruly but it shone with health. She didn't need beauty sleep. No amount of sleep would give her a more voluptuous figure or a smaller nose. Although, now that he was taking notice of her appearance, it occurred to him that her nose complemented her face, and her character, perfectly.

Her sister's face had even, well-proportioned features, but Daisy's face was a lot more interesting. As for her figure, well, since that was usually well disguised by loose-fitting clothes, he would just have to take her word on that.

Once inside, she switched on the PC, and

while it was booting up she went into the kitchen. 'What's your password?' he called, after a minute or two.

'What?'

'Your password. It won't go any further without it.'

She appeared in the doorway looking slightly flushed. 'I'll do it.' She crossed to the desk, edged him away from the keyboard. 'Turn away, then. It's supposed to be secret.'

'I'm not planning to come back at dead of night and steal all your secrets,' he protested.

'That's not the point.'

'I'll tell you mine if you tell me yours,' he offered. She waited for him to move and after a moment he shrugged and turned away, not fooled for a minute. It would be her lover's name, that was why she wouldn't let him see. He listened. Six keystrokes, then a return. Six letters. First name? Surname? First name. 'Okay, you can look now. It's pretty straightforward. You click on this to get e-mail, this to get on to the internet—'

'What about records? Does it store addresses, that sort of thing?'

'Of course it does. Here.' She clicked on an icon and got a list of files. 'Look, this is how you get the address book.' She clicked the mouse. 'See? It's all very simple—'

'Daisy, did you leave some milk on the stove?'

She stared at him for a moment. Then his words seemed to filter through and she turned and raced into the kitchen. By the time she'd returned, with two mugs on a tray and a pile of toast, he had helped himself to a blank disk from a box beside the computer, copied her address book and was apparently engrossed in surfing the net. 'I just saved it,' she said, putting the tray down on a small table.

'What?'

'The milk.' Then she grinned. 'I knew it. Men can never resist a new toy.'

'It's a good machine.' He logged off, closed it down, turned and saw the pile of buttery toast, spread thinly with Marmite. A nursery treat. 'Did anyone ever tell you that you're destined for sainthood?' She didn't look impressed. Well, he hadn't expected her to. That was one of the things he enjoyed about Daisy; she didn't take herself, or him, at all seriously. 'I think I'd better wash my hands.'

'Help yourself.'

Her bathroom was painted dark matt green, with an ornate gilded frame around the huge old mirror over the basin. There were fat little white and gold candles everywhere and the faint exotic scent of bergamot filled the small space. For just a moment Robert had a vision of Daisy lying back in the milky water of the bath, her fair skin translucent in the light of a dozen candles, her hair in soft damp curls about her face and shoulders. It was an image at once disturbingly sensual and faintly shocking and he took an involuntary step backwards. He'd never thought of Daisy in those terms before. As a woman.

Except why else was he there? His sole purpose for visiting her bathroom had been to look for evidence of a man in her life. But a quick search reassured him. There was nothing. Surely even the most careful man would leave some trace of his presence? A razor, a toothbrush? And wouldn't a woman in love cling to any small proofs that he belonged to her? His relief, though, was considerably soured by the discovery that spying on a friend did not make a man feel very good about himself.

He punished himself with the possibility

that Daisy's lover was too discreet to come to her flat. What had Michael said? Not much. Just that marriage appeared to be out of the question.

What the devil did that mean? Separated, maybe, and unable to divorce because of scandal? Someone well known? Was that what Michael had been hinting at. Whatever it meant, he'd already decided that while Michael might be too preoccupied with his wedding to do anything about the situation, he wasn't going to rest until he got to the bottom of it.

But he didn't linger. The disk in his jacket pocket was burning him like a brand and he was certain that guilt was written all over his face. 'I'll call you later in the week,' he said, making his excuses as soon as he could. 'Maybe we could have dinner.'

She seemed unusually reluctant to take him up on his offer. 'Can we leave it for now, Robert? I'm going to be rather busy this week.'

'That's the second time you've turned me down in as many days. I'm beginning to think there's something my best friend isn't telling me.'

'Oh, sure. Mr Insecure.' She gave him one

of those grins that made her look about ten years old. 'It's just I've got the sale this week, and the wedding...'

And fitting in a clandestine relationship, he thought. That must take a lot of time. Hanging about, hoping for a call. Always being available, just in case. She deserved better than that. 'You've got to eat,' he pointed out. 'And I was rather hoping you'd have some ideas for Michael's stag night.'

'Does a stag night require ideas? I thought all that was needed was buckets of alcohol, a sexy strippergram and a nearby lamp post for the ritual handcuffing of the bridegroom.'

'That's what you'd recommend, is it?'

'Far be it from me to defy convention.' She grinned. 'Ginny's having a hen night next week, and I promise you, we'll be doing it by the book. Frozen margaritas, TexMex food, and I have it on good authority that Zorro, or at least a reasonable facsimile, will be putting in an appearance.'

'Well, I'm shocked.' He made a good stab at looking shocked, but he could tell she wasn't convinced. 'You will tell me all about it afterwards, won't you?'

'You've got to be kidding. Unless you're

prepared to tell me what you get up to at Michael's party?'

'Ah.'

She laughed. 'Perhaps some things are best left to the imagination.' She crossed to the door. 'Time to go, Robert. You've had more than half an hour.'

'Times flies when you're having fun.' He bent to kiss her cheek and then, on an impulse, left the lightest of kisses on her mouth, sweetly bare of lipstick, instead.

She didn't speak, just looked at him, and her eyes were like the memory of a dream tugging at his consciousness but always just beyond his reach, a waking memory in which he was falling into huge, dark pupils, drowning in wide, silver fox eyes. Without warning he was fighting a desperate need to take her into his arms and kiss her the way she was made to be kissed, not in some hole in the wall hideaway by a mendacious man, but with a whole heart and total commitment. And for the second time that evening he found himself taking a step back.

Daisy closed the door and leaned against it. She was shivering, shaking so much that she clung to the doorknob with both hands. 'It

didn't mean anything. It didn't mean anything.' She whispered it over and over. He
was just being Robert. Kissing a woman
meant about as much to him as shaking
hands. It hadn't even been a real kiss. Just
one of those tokens between friends.
Meaningless. He'd kissed her once before,
just like that, and she'd been fooled into
thinking he meant it. Well, she'd been little
more than a child then. She wouldn't be
fooled again.

She tore herself away from the door and
went to gather the plates and mugs, put them
on a tray. But her hands were still shaking
too much. Everything was shaking too much.
Maybe she should turn up the heating.
Maybe she should take a hot bath.

It wasn't until she slid beneath the warm,
lavender-scented water that she stopped shivering for long enough to gather her wits and
promise herself that no matter what entice-
ments Robert held out to her, from now on
he would have to fill his own gaps. She had
no intention of seeing him again until the
wedding. None.

But it would be so much easier to believe
herself if her lips weren't still burning from
that meaningless kiss, if her body wasn't in

danger of instant conflagration. Hot bath. Cold shower. Nothing helped.

Robert slammed the disk into his PC and keyed in the instructions for his computer to print out a hard copy. Then he shut himself in the bathroom and tried to shower away the grubby feeling that he'd been left with after digging about in Daisy's personal life. It didn't work.

He wrapped a towel about his waist, gripped the basin and stared at his reflection in the mirror. He was doing it for *her*, he reminded himself. In the long run she would thank him, he knew she would. His reflection did not look convinced, so he covered his face with shaving foam and picked up a razor. Then he put it down again. He'd shave in the morning, when his hand was steadier.

His flat seemed very quiet. Janine had always had music playing when she was there, had always been on the telephone. He would have welcomed the peace, except that this time it simply meant the printer had stopped. That it was time to get on with the distasteful business of dissecting Daisy's private life.

First he poured himself a drink—he would need a drink to see him through the next hour or so—then gathered the sheets of paper spewed out by his printer before folding himself onto the sofa, glass in hand, and spreading them out across the low table.

She knew a lot of people, but quite a few could be ruled out straight away, he realised. The women, for a start. He paused, his pen above the first name. Women? A woman? For a moment everything suddenly seemed crystal-clear.

Then, with a very un-PC feeling of relief, he realised that couldn't be right. Michael had definitely said it was a man...a man she had been in love with for a very long time. How long was long? Where did they meet? How could he not have noticed? It was obvious that Michael knew who the man was, so why didn't he?

What had Michael seen that he had failed to notice? Whatever it was, Mike had made it quite clear that he wasn't going to tell, that he was on his own. Well, how hard could it be? He'd work on the process of elimination and whoever was left, no matter how improbable, had to be the answer. So he went through the list, crossing out all the women, then members of her family. Some of the men he knew and could rule out, too. His own name was there and he struck through that.

Of the remainder, three had names with six letters and, since he had to start somewhere, he circled them.

Samuel Jacobs had the distinction of offering a double six. The name suggested that he was Jewish, and if the family were Orthodox that might pose a bar to marriage, he supposed.

Conrad Peterson. The name sounded familiar, but the man lived in New Zealand and seemed an unlikely prospect.

The third name was Xavier O'Connell. Father Xavier O'Connell. And Robert's heart sank like a stone as he realised that the man was a priest. The ultimate impediment. He picked up his glass and then put it down again. That was not the answer.

He checked his watch. It was still short of eleven o'clock. Not too late to call a priest. And he picked up the telephone and dialled the number beside the name.

'St Catherine's. Can I help you?'

Robert hadn't expected a woman's voice, and it threw him for a moment. 'Er, may I speak with Father O'Connell, please?'

'It's rather late. Father O'Connell may

have retired for the night. Can he call you back in the morning?'

Late? Retired for the night? Tough. 'I'm afraid not. I need to speak to him urgently.'

'Then I'll go and see if he can come to the phone,' the voice replied, rather less eager to please now.

There was a pause, then a softly lilting Irish voice said, 'This is Father O'Connell. How can I help you?'

Robert gripped the receiver so hard that his knuckles whitened to the bone. 'Father O'Connell, my name is Robert Furneval. I'm a friend of Daisy Galbraith.'

'Robert Furneval?' The voice repeated his name thoughtfully. 'You'd be Jennifer's boy, I expect?'

He'd been expecting bluster, or stunned silence. Anything but this. 'You know my mother?'

'That I do. We met in Hong Kong twenty years or more ago, and a fine old time we had treasure-hunting for her bits and pieces, I can tell you. How is the dear woman?'

'Er... She's very well.'

'And Daisy? How is she? There's no problem, is there?' he added, a touch anxiously. 'She's not ill?'

'No. She's not ill.'

'Then maybe it's the translating you've called about? I'm doing it as fast as I can, but I'm afraid I'm not as young as I was. I was just fine until I reached eighty, but since then, well, my eyes aren't quite what they were and things seem to take longer than I expected.'

Robert swallowed. 'I'm sure she's happy to wait,' he said. And for once in his life he could think of nothing to say.

'And you, my son?' Father O'Connell prompted, quite gently. 'You have a problem?'

'Yes, Father, I do. But it seems that it isn't one that you can help me with after all. I'm very sorry to have troubled you so late.'

'Any time, dear boy. And tell Daisy to drop by for a glass of something warming very soon. Come yourself. This place is comfortable enough, but absolutely stuffed full with boring old men. I should know, I'm one of them.' And he chuckled. 'I'm always glad of some youthful company.'

St Catherine's, Robert realised, as he replaced the receiver, was not a church, but a home for retired priests. It was with a far lighter heart that he struck Xavier O'Connell's name from the list.

CHAPTER FIVE

MONDAY 27 March. Why on earth did Mike and Ginny decide to get married? No one gets married these days. Why didn't I think of going skiing? I could surely have managed to break something that wasn't totally immobilising...my nose would have been sufficient. Who'd want a bridesmaid with her nose in a splint? Painful, though...but not as painful as going to the hairdresser. And why did Robert kiss me?

'Well, this is going to be easy.'

Sitting in a Mayfair salon draped in vast swathes of pink and trying to avoid a reflection that was a particularly unhappy combination of darkly shadowed eyes and rather more damp little yellow curls than was quite decent, Daisy blinked.

'Easy?' No one had ever suggested that her hair might be easy.

The stylist smiled at her reflection. 'The

secret is not to fight the curls, but to use them,' he said.

'But I don't like curls. I want to have sleek, smooth, swishy hair like that girl on the shampoo ad on the television.'

His smile widened. 'Yeah, and I'd like to be six foot two and look like Robert Redford. We just have to make the best of what we've got, chick, and what you've got is thick, healthy hair.'

'And curls.'

'And curls,' he admitted. 'Learn to love them.'

Love them? That was an idea she hadn't encountered before. She'd been told since she was old enough to care that her hair was a disaster. She'd tried straighteners, a machine that was supposed to flatten the wildest curls, used every kind of conditioner on the market...

Love them? 'I think I'll need time to get used to that idea. In the meantime, I'll leave you to worry about them.'

'You do that. It's what I'm here for.' The stylist snipped as he chatted. 'I'll just tidy you up a bit.' Most hairdressers spoke to her soothingly, presumably hoping to avoid an explosion when they failed to provide the sleek locks demanded by her mother and for which she'd yearned throughout her teenage years. This man's confidence was like a breath of fresh air, and she began to relax as he trimmed the length a couple of inches, thinned out the sides a little, before, with a final ruffle of fingers through her hair, declared himself satisfied.

'That's it?' Actually it didn't look that much different, except that the mop of curls looked as if they had been planned that way, rather than lived with under sufferance. 'Aren't you going to do something excruciating with rosebuds?'

'Not today. A strand or two of ivy, a couple of well-placed white rosebuds on the day and that will be it. You'll look stunning.'

Stunning? That was kind of him, but she wasn't convinced. Her only hope was that she wouldn't look ridiculous next to the gorgeous brunettes. 'I wish I had your confidence.'

'You don't need it, you have my reputation. The photographs will be in the society magazines, and I promise, I'm not about to let you walk up the aisle behind the bride looking less than perfect.' He smiled at her as he whipped away the pink enfolding wrap.

'In the meantime, stop using those nasty rubber bands to tie back your hair. And it would be a big help if you'd get some sleep the night before the wedding, or, failing that, use some concealer to disguise those dark rings, or nobody will be looking at your hair.'

'Well, that's one solution.'

'But not the correct one.' He wasn't particularly amused by her flippancy. Maybe she was supposed to fling her arms about his neck and thank him for transforming her. Before she could make up her mind, he dismissed her with, 'Ask my receptionist and she'll give you some.'

The concealer might have dealt with the dark shadows, but it wasn't much help with the lack of sleep. Daisy's lids drifted heavily over her eyes as she sat at her desk, working her way through the sale catalogue in a determined act of concentration that allowed no room for her imagination to wander off to relive Robert's gentle kiss as it had done all through the long night. She woke with a start as her head hit the desk.

For a moment she wasn't quite sure what had happened, where she was. Then she rubbed her hand over her face and glanced at her watch. Lunchtime. Or rather time for her fitting. Maybe a walk across the park and a little fresh air would help.

Robert hadn't been able to get an answer from Samuel Jacobs on Sunday night and now he knew why. Mr Jacobs had apparently founded an import company in the nineteenth century to indulge the fashion for oriental artefacts, perishing without an heir when his ship had foundered in the South China sea. The company that bore his name survived, and was still importing works of art from the Far East, he discovered. However, he rather doubted that Daisy was in love with an import company, even one dealing in oriental antiques. Having crossed Samuel Jacobs from the list, he was at something of a loss.

He'd already eliminated the third possibility. Conrad Peterson had never seemed a likely candidate as Daisy's secret lover, but since the name had seemed so familiar he'd used the Internet to check him out. He was apparently a well-known collector, which was undoubtedly why Daisy had his name in her database, but his claim to fame was less esoteric. It was the size of the divorce settlement his wife had wrung from him when she'd found him in the marital bed with a man.

Damn Michael for being so coy. How did he expect him to help if he didn't give him something to go on? Except, of course, he hadn't asked him to help; that had been his own idea. He wondered if Ginny knew. He couldn't just call and ask her outright...he needed some excuse to talk to her. Better still, some reason for them to meet.

And he smiled as he remembered the promise he'd made Daisy.

'Ginny? Robert. I wonder if you could do something for me? I need about a metre of the yellow velvet your bridesmaids will be wearing.'

'How do you know about the yellow velvet? It's supposed to be a state secret.'

'I won't tell anyone. But only if I can have a metre.'

'That's blackmail. What do you want it for?'

'It's a surprise for Daisy.'

'It's a pleasant one, I hope.'

'Scout's honour. Can you drop it round to the office this afternoon? I'll give you a cup of Earl Grey and a chocolate biscuit and tell you all about it then.'

'I'll do what I can, but it had better be good.'

It was. Michael had no secrets from Ginny, but luring her to his office in order to pump her for information was just part of his plan.

He needed to see as much of Daisy as he could, and listen to her for a change, but she had been quite definite about being too busy to see him this week, what with hairdressers and fittings and hen nights. If he phoned her, he'd just get a polite brush-off. Somehow he had to get her to ring him.

He reached for a sheet of his personal notepaper, wrote a brief note, folded it and tucked it into an envelope, then addressed it to Daisy at the Latimer Gallery and headed for the door.

'Mary, I'm going out for a few minutes,' he informed his secretary.

'You've got a video conference with Delhi in half an hour,' she reminded him. 'And the Partners' lunch after that.'

'Would I miss the highlight of my week?'

'What's this?' Daisy regarded the white waxed box from a seriously expensive deli-catessen that was sitting on her desk when she returned with the black and gold box that contained the altered bridesmaid dress.

George shrugged. 'It arrived in a taxi about ten minutes ago. There's a note,' he added, quite unnecessarily; she had already picked up the thick square envelope that was sitting on top of the box.

Daisy recognised the writing at once and tried to remind herself that there was absolutely no reason for her heart to be fluttering in quite such a silly way. She had long ago stopped fluttering for Robert. Until last night. Since last night the fluttering had assumed volcanic proportions. She was fluttering right down to her fingertips.

She pushed a shaky thumbtip beneath the flap and flipped open the envelope, pulled out the single sheet of paper and unfolded it.

Dearest Daisy,
Since I am reliably informed that it is the best man's duty to take care of all the bridesmaids—not just the pretty ones—I have taken it upon myself to ensure that you don't miss lunch because of your dress fitting.
Robert.
PS Thanks for supper.

'The rat!' she exclaimed. 'Not just the pretty ones, indeed.' She dropped the note and opened the box. 'Oh!' The box contained the most exquisite arrangement of delicate little treats and she was forced to blink very hard.

'Supper?' George queried, picking up the note and scanning it as he helped himself to a tiny pastry stuffed with fresh salmon.

'Just Marmite soldiers and cocoa.'

'Really?' He licked his fingers. 'I should think the last woman who offered him that particular combination was his mother.' Then, 'I'd say you've definitely come out on top.'

'Have I?' She looked at the expensive array of delicacies. 'Yes, I suppose I have.' But if that was the case why did she suddenly have this weird sinking feeling? A hollow somewhere around her middle that her carefully ordered life was under attack. That Robert was up to something.

Damn Janine for getting clever a whole two weeks before the wedding and leaving Robert with a bigger gap than usual in his busy social life.

There was a time when she would have welcomed it, hugging the brief pleasure of his company close, storing up the memories as a squirrel stored nuts against the winter. But right now she didn't think she could take two whole weeks of such close attention without betraying herself. Not after that kiss.

She pushed the box nearer to George, so he could help himself more easily. She didn't feel in the least little bit like eating.

'Well? Aren't you going to phone him and say thank you nicely, the way your mother taught you?' His fingers hovered indecisively between another pastry and a piece of chicken. 'I'm sure he's sitting by his phone just waiting for your call.'

Her fingers were twitching, desperate for George to leave so that she could make that call, so that she could hear the sound of Robert's voice, perhaps discover the answer to the question that was plaguing her.

She was weakening, she realised with a shock. One kiss was all it had taken to jar loose the restraints she had placed around their relationship. One kiss. And with that realisation came the answer to her question. Robert was simply at a loose end and flirting came to him as naturally as breathing. She'd turned down his invitations twice in the same week and suddenly she was a challenge.

That was why he had kissed her, she realised angrily, and, having worked out what he was up to, not phoning him became very easy indeed.

She wasn't ever going to be one of his adoring girls, doing the predictable thing and falling at his feet. No way. Let him wait for her call. She directed her fingers in the safer direction of the chicken.

'Do you want that little asparagus tart, George, or are you going to finish the salmon?' she enquired, ignoring his question.

He gave her a thoughtful look and then shrugged. 'It's your lunch; you choose.'

'Just so long as we're both sure about that.' She ate the chicken and, discovering that she was hungrier than she had thought, she picked up a cherry tomato and firmly changed the subject. 'Now, I've had a final look at the sale catalogue and marked what I'd like to bid for with guide prices. Perhaps you'd better double check it.'

'Let's see.' He ran his eye over the list. 'You could go a little higher on a couple of items.' He marked them. 'What's this?'

'Oh, that's something Jennifer Furneval asked me to look at for her. You don't mind, do you?'

'Of course not, but I'll bet you anything you like that it's not Japanese. You know what to look out for?' He made a note beside the lot number without waiting for her answer. 'Of course you do. But no matter what Jennifer tells you, don't pay more than that.' He glanced up, his smile rueful. 'Unlike you, she's inclined to get carried away when she wants something very badly.'

'Five years from now it could seem like a bargain,' she pointed out.

'Yes, well, that's the risk. No one ever won the world by playing safe, my dear.' She had the feeling that he was saying a lot more than the words implied. Then he shrugged. 'But no one ever got burned, either. Maybe that's why we're dealers rather than collectors. Pragmatists, in it for a percentage rather than a lifetime commitment.'

Daisy glanced up. 'Are we still talking about porcelain?'

'What else?' His smile was so innocent that she almost believed him.

'Maybe, if it's a copy, I'll see something

else she'd like. Robert has been looking for a birthday present for her.'

'So long as you get the pieces I want, you can do what you like. Maybe even treat yourself. Did you manage to get a room at the Warbury Arms?'

'Any messages?' The Partners' lunch had seemed interminable, and while everyone around him had been full of the proposed merger, all he had been able to think about was Daisy and whether she had enjoyed her lunch.

Mary handed him a list of his calls along with a smart little black and gold carrier. 'A young lady called in with this.' She glanced at her notebook. 'Miss Ginny Layton. *Very* pretty—'

'And very early,' he said, checking his watch. 'No, I'm late. I wanted to speak to her, damn it.'

'She said she was sorry to miss out on the tea, but she's had a catering crisis that couldn't wait and she'd phone you later.'

'Ah, well, the best-laid plans...I wanted to pick her brains,' he added, when he saw Mary's cynical expression. 'She may be pretty, but since you'll undoubtedly have noticed the large diamond she's wearing on her left hand you'll have worked out for yourself that she's *very* engaged. In fact she's about to be married to my oldest friend.' He looked up from the list of messages she had given him. 'This is all? No one else called?'

'No one,' Mary confirmed. 'Maybe you're losing your touch, Robert. What's her name?'

'Daisy Galbraith...' He stopped. 'Oh, very funny. It's not like that; she's just an old friend.' Mary gave him an old-fashioned look. 'It's true. I've known her since she was in her highchair. If she calls you can ask her. But I'd rather you put her straight through. And in the meantime see if you can get hold of my mother.'

'It's *that* serious?'

'Serious?' Of course it was serious. Almost too late he realised that his secretary was still having a little fun at his expense and, recovering himself, he chided her softly. 'My dear Mary, when is it ever *that* serious?' Then he realised he was still holding the package. 'Have this sent over to my tailor, will you? He's expecting it.'

'Yellow velvet?'

'You peeked.'

'You didn't expect me not to, did you?' She waited expectantly for an explanation.

'It's material for a waistcoat. For the lovely Ginny Layton's wedding. I'm best man, and I thought it might be rather fun to match the bridesmaids' frocks.'

Mary chuckled at that. 'I'll bet you did. I'll bet the bridesmaids will think so, too. Velvet is so wonderfully touchy-feely—'

'My mother?' he reminded her, with just a touch of irritation. 'When you've quite finished being wittery-drooly.'

His mother wasn't at home, which on reflection, he decided, was probably just as well. If Mary assumed that his interest in Daisy was rather more than friendly, presumably anybody else he approached about her would take much the same view, but with rather less indulgence. And he wasn't in a position to defend himself against accusations of cradle-snatching.

Not that Daisy was in her cradle any more. Mike had rather forcefully made the point that she was twenty-four years old and a fully grown woman. Well, maybe she was, but he was light years older in experience, which was why he was eminently suited to the task of extricating her from whatever mess she was in. As her friend, it was his duty to extricate her from that mess.

Besides, the information he wanted was easily enough obtained by calling Monty Sheringham. There wasn't much point in having a contact on a national newspaper if you couldn't use him. He hadn't even needed to check with the Fine Arts correspondent; the sale Daisy was attending had to be the one at Warbury Manor; the family had provided Monty with many column inches in the past.

Since Daisy was going to be staying overnight, there seemed every likelihood that her lover would put in an appearance under the guise of visiting the sale on his own behalf.

Well, he would stay too. There was only one hostelry of any note in the village of Warbury, the Warbury Arms, and it had only one single room without bathroom available.

'It's the sale at the Manor,' the receptionist informed him apologetically.

'If it's all you have, I've no choice but to take it.'

He spent the rest of the afternoon, and quite a large part of the evening, clearing his diary and organising his office for his absence. It wasn't easy, and it was only when he reached home that he realised Daisy still hadn't called to thank him for her lunch. She must be very preoccupied to forget her manners, or very determined not to speak to him. But why?

He loosened his tie, switched on his answering machine and poured himself a drink. 'Robert?' Janine's voice floated teasingly across the room. 'Darling, I'm sorry to bother you, but have you found a scarf? Grey silk? I need it rather desperately. Call me if you have.'

He hadn't, but then he hadn't looked. Janine had waited longer than most to call, to give him a taste of missing her before offering a graceful opportunity to resume the relationship. But he had no capacity for commitment. Like father, like son. Nearly. His father was selfish; he'd wanted it all and his mother had paid the price. He wasn't about to do that to any woman. He'd look for the scarf and send it back by messenger.

The machine clicked. 'Robert, it's Ginny. I'm sorry I missed you today because I wanted to ask you do something for me. Something Mike said about Daisy make me think of it. I feel so guilty about pressuring her into standing in as bridesmaid, I know she hates the very idea, so I was wondering, would you look after her at the wedding for me? Make sure she has a good time? You're such an old friend and I can't think of anyone else who could do it half as well as you.'

'Flatterer,' Robert murmured wryly. 'Mike's a lucky man.' But what had Mike said to her? That was what he really wanted to hear.

'Robert.' At last. He checked the time of the message. Midafternoon, when she could easily have got him at the office. She was definitely avoiding him. Yet a warmth seeped into his veins at the sound of Daisy's voice. 'Thanks for lunch. It was a lovely thought and exactly what I needed after seeing myself in the finished dress. I'll see you at the wedding. You can't miss me, I'll be the ugly duckling on the left. Bye.'

He smiled, as no doubt she'd meant him to. 'I'll be looking out for you,' he promised. Then, more thoughtfully. 'In every sense.'

'Robert, would you do me a favour?' His mother's crisp voice brought him firmly back to earth as the next message clicked in. 'I asked Daisy to bid on a piece of porcelain for me at a sale this week, but never thought to organise some method of payment, and since it could be rather a lot of money I'd be grateful if you can ensure she won't be embarrassed for funds if she's successful? Bless you.'

He raised his glass in a salute to the machine. He'd been wondering how he was going to explain his presence at Warbury to a sceptical Daisy, especially since that 'I'll see you at the wedding...' had sounded suspiciously like a reprise of the 'don't call me...I'll call you' message he'd been getting from her.

'No, Mother, bless *you*, for giving me exactly the excuse I needed.'

CHAPTER SIX

TUESDAY 28 March. The train journey was hell, the viewing was mobbed and as for the rain!

George was right, of course. The Imari bowl isn't Japanese. There's something else, though, something I'd like to buy for Jennifer. Fat chance. I can't be the only person to have poked around in the kitchen boxes hoping to find something that might have been overlooked in the sheer quantity of crockery. Maybe I should have said something to one of the porters. It might get broken... Oh, hell!

Daisy kicked off her wet boots, shook out her raincoat and hung it, along with her umbrella, in the bathroom, before stripping down to her underwear. She'd never seen such rain!

She draped her trousers and sweater over the towel rail to dry out, and because the hotel wasn't one of those big chains that supplied all the trimmings, certainly not expensive accessories such as bathrobes, she slipped into the Chinese silk wrap she'd brought with her. Then, taking a hand towel, she curled up into an elderly chintz-covered armchair while she dried the drips from her hair.

She'd felt guilty about the cost of a double room when she'd booked, but it had been the only decent room they'd had left, and after a day poking about the treasures, and the junk, collected by generations of the Warbury family, a day when the rain had come down like stair rods without ceasing, she knew she deserved it.

The first day of a Harrods sale would never seem like hard work again, she decided as she wiggled her aching toes and tried to summon up the energy to make herself a cup of tea. But her energy was on go-slow and her gaze shifted to the mini-bar. Would there be a brandy?

She thought about how blissfully warm it would feel sliding down her throat and decided to check it out. In a minute. Right now she just wanted to close her eyes. Just for a moment or two. Then she'd look.

*   *   *

The Warbury Arms was a mellow old country inn, all oak-panelling, open fires and copper warming pans, the very image of Olde Englande so beloved of tourists, and in this case, Robert could see, it was the genuine article.

The rain was genuine, too, and he had to push his way through a steaming crowd of dealers and collectors gathered for the sale just to get to the reception desk.

'Has Miss Galbraith checked in?' he asked, raising his voice against the babble as he signed the register.

'Miss Galbraith?'

Robert had assumed she would be staying close to the Manor, but, looking around at the heaving crowd, it occurred to him that she might have chosen somewhere quieter. Somewhere more discreet. 'She's with the Latimer Gallery.'

'Oh, yes, of course. She came in a few minutes ago. Will you be dining together? I'd advise booking a table; we're very full.'

'I'll see what she wants to do and let you know.' It was entirely possible that she had other plans and would not be at all pleased to see him. The thought was so depressing that for just a moment he considered turning around and going home. But only for a moment. Michael might choose to look the other way, but he couldn't. 'What's her room number?'

It took him less than ten minutes to dump his bag in his room and freshen up and then he went in search of Daisy. Her room was at the front of the hotel and he paused for a moment before he knocked. He had his excuse all ready, but he still hesitated, feeling just a little like some cheap private eye in an old movie hoping to catch the guilty husband *in flagrante*.

He bunched his fist and laid it against the door. Confronting Daisy like this wasn't what he would have chosen. The desk clerk hadn't mentioned anyone else, but that didn't mean she was alone and he had no wish to embarrass her, or catch her out. He just wanted to help. Before he could do that, though, he needed information.

Maybe he should go downstairs and wait for her to come down. That would be kinder. Except maybe she wouldn't come down. Maybe it would be room service and champagne. Maybe he was just a coward.

He hadn't thought much about what he would do if she was with someone; he was certain that she would be embarrassed and he didn't want that. They were friends, the best of friends, and his concern for her was very real. Then he remembered the way her eyes had looked in that moment after he had kissed her. The way he had wanted to do a lot more than kiss her. And suddenly he didn't feel like being kind. He had to know.

He rapped on the door. There was no answer.

Maybe, he told himself, she was in the bath. Maybe she was, right now, deep in concentration in some reference book, swotting up for the sale and refusing to be disturbed. A week ago he would have expected nothing else, but it had been a long week and maybe, he thought, maybe she was lying in the embrace of her secret lover...

He brought his knuckles down hard against the old panelled door.

Daisy woke with a start. For a moment she wasn't sure where she was or what had woken her. Then she lifted her head, pushed her hair out of her eyes and checked her watch, wondering if she'd slept all night in the chair. It felt like it, but she'd been there for less than half an hour. She shivered a little and yawned.

Then was a knock at the door, loud enough to suggest that it wasn't the first. She sighed, hauled herself out of the chair and, assuming that it was the maid coming to turn down the sheets, she opened the door.

'Hello, Daisy.'

'Robert!' Usually she had time to gather herself, prepare herself, but caught unawares she took an involuntary step back, over-whelmed by his unexpected appearance. Taking it as an invitation, he followed her into the room.

Robert hadn't known what to expect, but Daisy, tousled, sleepy-eyed and wearing a thigh-length silk wrap, knocked him for six. His mouth dried, and any pretence that this was anything but personal flew out of the window. His only thought was to take her in his arms and carry on where he had left off on Sunday night.

Or was even that only half the story? Wasn't the whole truth that he hadn't been able to get Daisy out of his head since Monty's party? Hadn't the little green-eyed monster leapt on his shoulder the moment he saw her with Nick Gregson? Even now his eyes were everywhere.

'This is comfortable. Big for one, though.'

'There wasn't much choice,' she said defensively. 'It was this or an attic without a bathroom. Robert, what on earth are you doing here?'

'I'm on a mission.' He crossed to the tray, where there was a kettle for making hot drinks. The kettle was cold and empty and he glanced around, looking for the bathroom. Looking for any sign of dual occupancy. A man's jacket lying over the chair, the telltale shoes. Nothing. Relief was short-lived. After all it was early. Maybe it wasn't shock he had seen in her face, but disappointment. 'Any chance of some tea?' he asked.

'I was just trying to decide between tea or brandy when I fell asleep,' she confessed, dragging her fingers through her hair and stifling a yawn. 'What kind of mission?'

'It's too early for brandy.'

'Probably, but it's been a hell of a day. Here, give that to me before I weaken,' she said, taking the kettle into the bathroom to fill from the tap. 'What kind of mission?' she repeated, calling out to him.

'Maybe "mission" is putting it too strong.

More an errand of mercy. I'm here to keep you company, buy you dinner...' She appeared in the bathroom doorway looking sweetly dishevelled, her short robe displaying a pair of remarkably long, slender legs. And he remembered the long-limbed child racing after Mike, racing after him when he was a boy and desperate to escape her hero-worship. Her legs had always been long and slender; that was why her knees had seemed so large. The memory made him smile.

'What's so funny?'

'What? Oh, nothing.' And the smile faded as quickly as it had come. The legs had shape now, and her knees were just fine. 'You've done something to your hair,' he said, simply to distract himself.

'I told you I was seeing the wedding stylist. He didn't do much, just snipped a bit off. Clearly he decided I wasn't worth the effort. Why are you here, Robert?'

'You didn't believe me about dinner?'

'Er, let me see. No,' she said, without even hesitating. Then she carried the kettle across to the tray. 'No one in their right mind would come out in this weather unless they had to.'

'That's true.'

'Are you saying you had to come?'

'Direct orders. I had a message on my answering machine asking me get down here with my chequebook.' He took the kettle from her, plugged it in and switched it on before turning to face her. 'You're buying something for my mother?' he prompted. 'She thought you might need some money.'

'Oh.' Then, 'Oh, dear. I'm sorry, Robert, but you've had a wasted journey. The bowl your mother was interested in is just a copy.'

It was the excuse that had interested him, not the bowl. But she seemed disappointed. 'It was a fake?'

'No, a copy. The designs were copied by everyone. Some porcelain was even imported unfinished from Japan and then decorated in Europe. The bowl in the sale is listed simply as "Imari-style porcelain"; I guess the maker's mark was removed at some time by someone hoping to pass it off as Japanese. It might fool an amateur, but Jennifer wouldn't be interested.'

'Damn. I'd hoped to give it to her as a birthday present.'

'I was going to suggest it, if it had been what she wanted.'

'Well, maybe there's something else?'

'Maybe.'

Robert's eyes narrowed. Daisy was tired. She had dark smudges beneath her eyes that he'd never seen before, but there was nevertheless a sparkle about her, an edge of excitement that he doubted had anything to do with the sale. It made him feel quite sick, and he turned away, dropped a couple of teabags in the cups provided.

'I'll see what I can find. How much are you prepared to spend?' she asked.

He shrugged. 'Whatever it takes. I'll know when I see it.'

'See it?'

'Of course. Now I'm here, I might as well stay for the sale.'

'Oh.' For a moment Daisy had been tempted to tell him about the Kakiemon dish she'd spotted in a box of assorted kitchen china. She'd hoped to buy it for Jennifer herself, but it would make a wonderful birthday present for Robert to give her. If she could get it at a reasonable price. But you could never tell how even the most level-headed person would react at a sale, and she didn't want to take the risk of his excitement giving away her find. If she *was* right about it. 'Where are you staying?'

'In the attic without the bath that you turned down, I imagine,' Robert replied.

'Don't be silly. Haven't you seen the crowds downstairs? There won't be a room available within ten miles of this place.'

Robert realised she had misunderstood him, but he didn't enlighten her. If he *had* jumped the gun, and her lover was arriving later, it might be better if she thought him safely out of the way. Still it wouldn't hurt to tease her a little. In fact, she would expect it. 'Well, you've got a spare bed,' he said, indicating the twin beds with a night table separating them. Not his first choice for a night of passion. 'You wouldn't send me out into the rain, would you?'

'You won't dissolve.'

'Maybe not, but if I don't get out of these wet socks very soon I'll probably catch cold.'

'Pneumonia. You need a virus to catch cold.'

'Pneumonia? Do you think so? With a cold I might just make it as best man. I'd give it to all the guests, of course, but with pneumonia...' He left her to fill in the gap.

'And of course without you Michael and

Ginny would definitely have to cancel the wedding,' she said, then grinned. 'Not.'

The exchange was the usual jokey banter between friends, but he detected an edge to her voice. A nervousness. So, the spare bed was already spoken for and three would be a crowd. It was only what he had expected and yet a kind of impotent rage seemed to grip him. He had to *know*. 'I suppose I could drive back to Ross and find a room there, but there's no reason we couldn't have dinner first,' he said, pushing her the way he'd worry a sore tooth.

'Actually, Robert, I'd planned to have a sandwich up here and get an early night.' And she curled up in the big armchair as if to convince him.

'On your own?' The words just slipped out.

'Go back to London, Robert. I'll find something for Jennifer's birthday; you can pay me when you see me.'

He shrugged. She hadn't appeared to notice the implication behind his words. Or she was very good at hiding her feelings.

Private. That was what Michael had said. She was very private.

'You wouldn't begrudge me a cup of tea

before you throw me out, would you?' He didn't wait for an answer, but poured the boiling water onto the teabags. 'There, just like Mother makes,' he said, adding the milk and passing her a cup. Then, looking down at her, curled up into the big armchair, her thick mane of curls tumbled loose about her face, he said, 'You know, you shouldn't worry about your knees. They're not in the least bit knobbly.'

She tugged self-consciously at the short wrap she was wearing, trying to cover them, and something inside him boiled up and was in danger of bubbling over. Why on earth was she so coy around him? Her legs weren't exactly a mystery to him. He'd seen her more times than he could remember in a skimpy swimsuit when they'd all swum in the river. He and Michael and Daisy. It had been something they had done every summer until he'd gone away to university. No, later than that. Until he'd graduated and moved to London.

'What time does the fun start?' he asked sharply.

'Fun?'

She looked startled. Guilt? 'Tomorrow. The sale,' he said.

'Oh, I see. I wouldn't have described it as fun, exactly, but there's an hour for viewing in the morning and then the sale starts at ten. 'With luck and a kind train schedule, I should be home by five.'

'Won't someone offer you a lift?'

'I never accept lifts from strangers,' she said.

'Maybe you'll see someone you know.' He finished his tea, put down his cup and crossed to the door. 'If I stayed I could take you myself,' he said, offering a lure.

She wasn't to be hooked. 'You'd get bored,' she said. 'It won't be like those dramatic sales you see on the news, with paintings going for millions.'

'I have been to a sale before. Sure you won't change your mind about dinner?'

She got up, followed him to the door. 'Quite sure. Thank you.'

Robert looked down at her, saw something very like desperation darkening her eyes, and because he cared so much about her he reached out, touched her cheek, forced his mouth into the kind of smile she would be expecting. 'You know, I'm beginning to think you're trying to get rid of me, duckling.

You haven't got a secret lover hiding in the bathroom, have you?'

'Damn, you've found me out,' she said, and suddenly laughed, neat white teeth in bright contrast to warm lips, lips that were sweeter and more inviting than he could ever have imagined. But then, as she looked at him, her eyes misted over. 'Please drive carefully,' she said quickly. And, putting her hand on his shoulder to steady herself, she lifted herself onto her toes and kissed his cheek. Her hand on his shoulder, her soft breath against his skin left his immovable centre spinning out of control.

A week ago he would have laughed the thought of Daisy with a secret lover to scorn. Now he couldn't get the idea out of his head, and he glanced at the bathroom door, shut carefully after she had filled the kettle, and wondered if he had inadvertently stumbled on the truth.

For a moment Daisy leaned back against the door and groaned. Damn George for being so knowing. Damn Jennifer for being so thoughtful. Damn Robert for making her love him and for being so far out of reach... She groaned again.

Damn him, but she couldn't do it. She couldn't send him out into a black, wet night. She wouldn't do it to a dog, much less a man she loved, just to save herself from pain. Because sharing a room platonically with him was her idea of a nightmare. It wasn't as if he would even think of making a move on her. She'd be quite safe.

Lucky her.

She wrenched open the door, ready to call him back, but the corridor was empty. 'Damn!' She pushed her feet into her still damp boots and without stopping to tie the laces grabbed her key and, banging the door shut behind her, raced to the stairs before she quite lost her nerve.

'Robert!' He was halfway down the stairs when he turned and saw her, and for a moment stood quite still.

'What is it, duckling?'

'I, er, I changed my mind about dinner,' she said, suddenly aware that she was attracting rather a lot of attention from the bustle of men and women who had spilled out of the overcrowded bar and were filling the reception area, glasses in their hands.

Robert's quick smile distracted her. 'Just dinner?'

She flushed. 'Jennifer would never forgive me for sending you out on a night like this when there's a spare bed going begging.'

She waited, expecting him to say something silly to put her at her ease. Instead he came back up the stairs, took her hand and held it for a moment. Then he said, 'Why don't you go and put some clothes on while I book a table?'

Clothes? For a moment Daisy wasn't quite with him, then she realised that she was standing above a room full of people wearing nothing but a thigh-length wrap. A thigh-length wrap and a pair of brown ankle-high laced boots. Oh, wow. Great. Without waiting to answer him, she grabbed the edges of her wrap tightly about her and walked carefully back up the stairs. She would have liked to run, but this was not the moment to risk tripping over her trailing laces.

Behind her she heard a sudden bubble of laughter and she groaned. The dealers' world was such a small one. Today she had been able to poke about the trivia of the sale without anyone taking much notice of her. With one impulsive gesture she had made herself the centre of attention, and thirty years from now people would still be saying, 'Daisy

Galbraith? I know her. I was at Warbury when she chased some man through the bar half-naked...' Antique dealers were like fishermen—they never spoiled a good story by sticking strictly to the truth.

She banged the door shut behind her. Why on earth couldn't she have just done the sensible thing? she asked herself. She was good at sensible. She'd been doing sensible very successfully since she was sixteen years old, when she'd realised that she had two choices. Let Robert Furneval break her young heart, or keep it firmly under lock and key.

Why did she have to lose her head now?

Before she could offer a sensible answer, she caught sight of herself in the cheval mirror and instead she shuddered. Too much leg, too much everything, and most of it flushed a revolting shade of embarrassment pink that clashed horribly with her yellow hair.

The very thought of going back down to the bar filled her with deep embarrassment. Maybe they could have room service? But that would be even worse. That would mean spending the whole evening alone with Robert in a bedroom. What would they do? What would they talk about? And then there would be the awkwardness of changing for bed...she'd bet pounds against pretzels that he didn't wear pyjamas.

If they were downstairs, she could make some excuse to come up first and be safely tucked beneath the covers with her eyes tightly closed before he climbed into bed. If she was quick, she could be properly dressed before he returned.

She eased her feet out of her damp boots and opened the wardrobe. There wasn't much choice. She wasn't a 'pack-for-every-occasion' girl. She had never seen the point of carrying more than she needed. She'd worn a pair of old, but serviceable trousers for rooting around the Manor, the kind of garment that wouldn't crease and wouldn't show the dust and at a pinch, with a silk blouse, would take her through to dinner. Or would have, if she hadn't dashed through a rainstorm and stepped in a puddle that had seemed to reach her knees.

So that only left the sharp little suit that, bearing George's instructions not to let the gallery down, she had decided to wear to the sale. And the shoes with five-inch heels that she had bought to go with it. She had rather relished the idea of distracting a rival bidder by crossing her legs at just the right moment.

Well, she'd distracted them, all of them, and she hadn't even needed the heels. It was just her timing that was off.

What she wouldn't have given for a long, anonymously grey skirt right now, and the sensible low-heeled shoes she'd taunted George with.

But something warned her that as far as this buying trip went she might as well strike the word 'anonymous' from her dictionary, and with that uncomfortable thought for company, she went to take a shower.

Robert wasn't sure how he was feeling. A little numb. In a minor state of clinical shock, perhaps.

He'd left Daisy's room in a mood that had bordered on misery. That alone should have been sufficient to alert him that he was heading for trouble. But then he'd turned at the sound of her voice calling his name, seen her a few feet above him wrapped in thin red silk that barely covered her thighs, her cheeks picked out in a pale pink flush... Well, most of the occupants of the Warbury Arms were probably in a state of shock, too. But it hadn't been the wrap, or the legs that had done it for him. He'd seen them just moments before, without the ardour-dampening effect of the boots.

It had been the heart-leaping sense of joy at what her change of heart meant. And then the equally rapid descent into somewhere very like hell as Michael's words had echoed in his mind. *There's a man she's been in love with for a very long time...* She might be alone tonight. Maybe he couldn't get away tonight. But there *was* someone.

Well, maybe it was for the best. The very idea of Robert Furneval falling in love was so ridiculous, so dangerous that he should be laughing. Instead, for the first time in his life, he felt more like crying at the cruel lack of something precious in his character, something that made falling in love with Daisy an impossibility. And the urge to protect her from heartbreak, seen for the selfishness at its heart, was suddenly grotesque.

He'd confess to the attic, stay over and give her a lift home. She deserved no less from him. Then he'd do what she wanted and stay away from her until the wedding. Hopefully Fiona, or Maud or Diana would provide sufficient distraction after that. It shouldn't take long to get over her if his usual attention span was anything to go by, he thought bitterly.

'I'd like to book a table for dinner,' he said to the reception clerk. 'For two.'

'Seven or nine o'clock, sir? We're having to double-stack the tables, tonight.'

'Seven—' he began, then turned as a middle-aged woman beside him raised a desperate voice.

'But you must have a room! I'll take anything. My car has broken down and there's absolutely no chance of getting it fixed until tomorrow.' She was soaking wet, exhausted and clearly at her wits' end.

'You can have my room,' Robert said. 'Twenty-three,' he added as the room clerk raised his eyebrows. 'I can double up with a friend.' The woman turned to thank him, but he cut her short. 'It's not a problem. I'll go and move my bag and bring the key.'

Not a problem. Not much. At least his good deed had wiped out the lie he'd told Daisy. Now all he had to do was live with the consequences.

She'd left the door on the latch for him; he could hear the shower running in the bathroom and he tapped on the door to let her know that he was there. 'Can I pour you a drink?'

The shower stopped. 'Er, yes. Thanks. I'll be out in a minute.'

'No rush.' He could do with a few minutes to gather himself.

He examined the mini-bar, found a brandy for Daisy and Scotch for himself and split a bottle of ginger ale between the two, and was very carefully watching the rain splashing onto the porch below when she opened the door.

'Is this mine?'

'Brandy and ginger. It'll warm you up.' And he half turned. His discretion was unnecessary. She had a towel around her hair, a bath sheet covering her from armpit to ankle and her wrap worn loosely over that. What remained visible was rather pink, and it occurred to Robert that the last thing Daisy needed was warming up.

'I'll take this through to the bathroom with me,' he said, picking up his glass. 'We haven't got long; I said we'd eat at seven. I thought you'd want an early night.' And suddenly his own face felt a touch on the warm side. 'After such a long day.'

'Seven o'clock is just fine.'

He closed the bathroom door behind him and allowed himself a momentary image of Daisy dashing about the bedroom, getting into her clothes and make-up in record time so that she'd be ready when he emerged. The thought provoked a welcome smile and he sipped at his drink, listening for the telltale sounds.

What he heard was the quiet ting of the telephone as she lifted the receiver to make a call.

CHAPTER SEVEN

TUESDAY night or Wednesday morning. It doesn't matter. All that matters is that I've been stupid. Thoroughly stupid. Robert's a grown man with the kind of car that would laugh in the face of bad weather, but I had to come over all melodramatic and conscience-ridden and now he's lying three feet away from me. Almost near enough to touch, and it's so quiet that I can hear him breathing. I can't bear it!

And as if that's not bad enough, everyone is going to know we spent the night together.

Daisy heard the bathroom door close. In a minute she'd hear the shower and then there would be nothing in her head but Robert. Robert standing naked beneath the spray, water glistening on his skin, dripping from his hair, running down his thighs… She snatched up the telephone, desperate for a distraction, any distraction.

'Hello, Daisy.' George Latimer had picked

up the telephone so quickly that she suspected he'd been waiting for her to call. 'What kind of day have you had?'

'Long, cold and wet, but that's par for the course.'

'No problems, then?'

Problems? Ha! 'Not a problem, exactly.' The British talent for understatement was safe in her hands.

'Oh? Well, if it's not a problem, perhaps you'd better tell me what, "exactly", it is.'

How about Robert Furneval turned up this evening and right now he's in my bathroom—naked—and later on, we're going to be sleeping together? Well, not together, but in the same room, which is near enough to be a serious problem. That's what 'exactly' is... 'Well, the thing is, George, I think I might have spotted something rather special...'

'I don't suppose for a moment it's what you think it is, Daisy,' he said, when she'd explained at length about the dish she'd found amongst the kitchen china. 'It's so easy to get carried away.' Carried away? She was the least likely person to get 'carried away' that she knew. Suppression could be her middle name. Which was why she wasn't in the shower and naked herself right now. 'Finds like that are rarer than hen's teeth, you know.' George's voice wrenched her back to reality.

'But not unknown?' she persisted. Priceless bowls had been discovered being used to feed some pampered pooch.

'Not unknown,' he agreed, but she could almost *hear* his shrug. 'But don't let desire for glory run away with your common sense.'

'You think I should forget it, then?'

'Unless you want a box of banqueting size kitchen china. You're a professional, not a bargain hunter.'

'But if I'm right?'

'Why are you calling me, Daisy? I can't authenticate a piece of porcelain over the telephone. Use your best judgement.'

She hadn't been asking for his opinion on its authenticity. That wasn't her dilemma. She knew what she'd seen. 'That wasn't why I rang. I just wondered if I should mention it to the auctioneers.'

She had half expected him to question her sanity. Instead he considered her question and then said, 'Well, I suppose you could.' He sounded doubtful.

'But you don't advise it.'

'I'm thinking of you, my dear. If you're right, they'll look stupid, and they won't enjoy the experience and they won't forget it, either. And neither will anyone else. You'll be followed round sales for evermore by reporters, dealers, just about anyone looking for a bargain or a story. Of course, if you're wrong, you'll be the one with egg on your face and they'll have a good laugh at your— and Latimer's—expense.'

'But what about the seller?'

'You're a dealer, Daisy. If the auctioneers haven't spotted something interesting, it's not your concern.'

'I know, but—'

'The present Baronet has inherited all his family's talent for wasting money, in his case gambling, drink and expensive women. Anything left after the sale will undoubtedly go the same way.' Having dealt with the Warburys, he changed the subject. 'Are the lots we discussed up to scratch?'

After they'd discussed the items she was to bid for and she'd hung up, she realised that she'd got what she wanted. George had distracted her with a vengeance. In fact his dismissal of her opinion had seriously irritated her.

She pulled the towel from her hair and fluffed it with her fingers. She'd buy the box of china and jolly well show him, and if she'd made a mistake, well, she knew a caterer who would be more than happy to take good dishes off her hands. And if the dish was genuine, well…she wouldn't be rubbing anyone's nose in her find, so that wouldn't be a problem.

She was in her lacy black teddy, sitting at the dressing table painting on her lipstick, when the bathroom door clicked open. 'Are you decent?'

Not particularly. She'd planned to be dressed, buttoned up to the neck and waiting at the door to bolt the moment he emerged from the bathroom. But he'd think her modesty funny, and after George's casual dismissal of her ability, she wasn't in the mood to be laughed at.

'Compared with my recent appearance in Reception wearing next to nothing and a pair of boots, I'd say I was probably overdressed.' He didn't answer and she turned her head. He was leaning against the bathroom door, wearing a bathsheet tucked around his waist and nothing else. Not even a smile. Well, that was all right, then.

Except that his dark hair was slicked back from the shower and a tiny spot of shaving foam clung to his jaw, lending an almost unbearable intimacy to his presence in her room.

It was a long time since she'd seen Robert without a shirt and time had only improved him. His chest had broadened and was now spattered with a shadow of dark hair that arrowed towards his waist. His shoulders were wider and his arms strong and sinewy. This was the body hinted at by the golden youth she had fallen in love with, and her mouth momentarily dried at the sight of him. Then, when he still said nothing, she swallowed and found her voice. 'What is it?'

'I never quite saw you as the kind of girl who would wear black underwear.'

'Really?' From some unexpected reserve of strength she managed sarcasm. 'So you've thought about it?' Actually, she didn't want to know that, and before he could answer, she added. 'Strange, I've never given your underwear a moment's thought.'

Liar, liar, pants on fire. You've thought about it, Daisy Galbraith. Black cotton box-

ers. Black close-fitting briefs. Or those soft clinging shorts that left nothing to the imagination. In black. She could never quite make up her mind.

She forced herself to turn away, blot her lipstick, then stand and walk across to the wardrobe. She was conscious of his gaze following her every movement as she took down her suit, stepped into the skirt and fastened it at the waist.

It was too short. Far too short. She felt naked in it. She slipped into the neat little jacket and fastened the buttons. It didn't help much. She turned and picked up the drink he had poured for her and which she had barely touched.

It was both hot and cold, the sharpness of the ginger cooling the back of her throat, the brandy warming her from the inside out as it spread through her system. It made her feel a little light-headed. Something was making her feel light-headed.

Robert finally moved, opened his bag and shook out a dark red shirt, a tie. She held her breath. His shorts were the soft clinging kind. But white. Surprises all round, then. He retreated to the bathroom and shut the door.

* * *

In the safety of the bathroom, Robert finally let out a long-held breath. He had doubted Mike when he'd said his little sister was a grown woman. Mike must have thought he was out of his mind. Or blind. Or both.

Dear God, what had he been doing while Daisy was growing up? Why hadn't he noticed how much she had changed? Because he'd never seen her looking like that before? Or maybe he just hadn't been looking.

Or maybe she hadn't wanted him to see.

No. That was ridiculous. Yet there was no denying the fact that she was like some Jekyll and Hyde character. One side of her the casual, friendly Daisy that he'd always known and had come racing to Warbury like some latter-day Galahad to protect. The girl who'd come to lunch whenever he was at a loose end, the girl who'd sit quietly all day on a riverbank, dangling her toes in the river, and who never took herself too seriously. But apparently there was another side.

Elegant, slightly distant and sexy as sin. The woman who had sat at her dressing table in black silk underwear, blotting her lipstick, knew exactly what she was doing. She was a woman with creamy shoulders and a long, sensuous waist and small, high breasts that for once were not hidden beneath layers of clothing but clearly etched by a trimming of fine black lace.

She was a woman with a secret lover, and one who clearly didn't need anyone to protect her.

His fingers shook slightly as he fitted cuff-links into his shirt. He shouldn't have done this. He shouldn't be here. But he'd burned his boats roomwise and, unless he was prepared to drive home through torrential rain, here he'd have to stay. Maybe the rain was safer.

The lightning flash that lit up the small frosted window pane swiftly followed by a threatening rumble of thunder suggested otherwise, and he wasn't a fool. Not much.

Yet still he lingered in the bathroom. Until today he'd never had to think about what he might say to Daisy. Conversation had been easy, unforced. Now he didn't even begin to know what to say to her. What would they talk about? How would they spend an evening in trivial conversation, teasing one another in the way they always had, when his mind had a completely different agenda.

The wedding, he thought, clutching at straws. They could talk about the wedding.

No. Oh, God no. Anything but white-lace-and-promise talk. That would remind him too painfully of what he could never have. What he had never, until this moment, wanted.

Neutral. He needed something neutral to talk about. And, taking a deep breath, he opened the bathroom door. 'Right,' he said, as he pulled on his jacket. 'If I'm going to this sale tomorrow you're going to have to educate me. I don't want to walk out of there tomorrow with a stuffed parrot under my arm.'

Daisy laughed on cue as he opened the bedroom door and ushered her through it, determined to get them both into the safety of the public area as quickly as he could. 'I thought you said you'd been to one of these things before.'

'I have. I was rising seven and my father made me sit on my hands through the entire day.'

'Your father?' She glanced at him in surprise. 'Is he a collector, too? Jennifer never mentioned it.'

'That's because he wasn't. Isn't. He's a historian. His area is social history and his interest was purely intellectual. Poking about in the lives of families who'd lived in the same place for generations. He met my mother at a sale.'

'Did he?' He rarely mentioned his father and Daisy seemed lost for words. 'You must have been bored to death,' she said finally.

'No.' To have his father to himself for a whole day had been worth the agony of sitting still, keeping quiet. 'He took me out to lunch, gave me a glass of watered-down wine and let me eat what I liked.' And he'd flirted with one of the pretty waitresses. With the twenty-twenty vision of hindsight, and an adult's knowledge of human behaviour, it seemed probable that his father's sole purpose in visiting the restaurant had been to meet with the waitress, the freedom of the menu and the glass of wine the simplest way to distract his son.

'Do you ever see him?'

'My father? Occasionally. When he's between affairs he's deluded into thinking my mother is the only woman he's ever truly loved, so he invites me to dinner and tries to persuade me to intervene with her, on his behalf.'

'And do you?'

'There's no point. He has an attention span where women are concerned roughly similar to that of a goldfish. If he cared enough he'd make the effort himself.' He turned as they reached the stairs. Was it his imagination or did she seem taller? He glanced down and realised that it was no illusion. Daisy was wearing seriously high heels.

Janine had worn shoes like that. They'd cost a fortune, but she'd taken the view that for jaw-dropping sex appeal there was nothing to beat them and he'd agreed with her. But that was Janine and this was Daisy. Daisy, who wore sensible shoes and jeans or long skirts over boots. Daisy, who tied her hair back in elastic bands. At least she did when she was with him.

He stopped. 'What happened to the boots?'

'They're stuffed with newspaper and drying out,' she said, and, realising that he was staring at the exquisite black peep-toe shoes that she was wearing, she put her feet neatly together and looked down at them too. It must have been to disguise the sudden rise of colour to her cheeks, because she presumably knew what they looked like. 'George recommended these,' she said, before moving off with that hip-lifting swing that very high heels demanded. 'He expects me to use them to distract the opposition.'

'It works for me.'

'Oh, this is nothing.' She giggled, as if she'd remembered something slightly wicked. 'Just wait until I cross my legs. I've been practising in the mirror.'

That he refused to believe, but he forced himself to smile back. Keep it light. 'Are you *determined* to cause a riot here tonight?'

'Now that's a thought. If all these hard-nosed dealers think I'm just a blonde airhead, they won't take me very seriously tomorrow, will they?'

'Don't you want them to take you seriously?'

'Not tomorrow.'

Daisy saw the doubt in Robert's eyes. Well, she'd have to try harder. If she could convince him that this Daisy was the pretend one, she might have salvaged something from the mess.

'With luck,' she added, 'I might get away with it for quite some time. Will you help?'

He looked somewhat startled. 'If I can. What do you have in mind?'

Think...think... 'Well, you've known lots of girls—'

'Are you suggesting I'm a serial airhead fancier?'

'Would I do that?' Daisy widened her eyes in a terrific impression of the fluffiest of girls and she laid her fingertips lightly against her breast to emphasise her point. 'I think Janine was really quite clever.'

'Only *quite* clever?'

'Well, she was clever enough to jump before she was pushed. But if she had been really smart she'd have been planning her own wedding right now.' Her smile invited him to laugh at himself. 'Wouldn't she?'

Robert chuckled obligingly, but Daisy had the feeling his heart wasn't in it. 'You know, for a duckling, you're really quite bright.'

'Shh. That's a state secret.' Then, because she'd seen airheads in action, she giggled again.

'Don't overdo it, sweetheart,' he warned.

'Is that possible?'

'Cat.' That was better. They were back to trading casual insults, and her spirits lifted a little as they paused in the entrance to the dining room. 'I'm afraid we didn't get as much head-turning attention crossing Reception as you deserve.' His voice had just the right amount of edge, Daisy was glad to note. The words might have been right, but he hadn't been paying her a compliment.

He was right, though; the crowds had thinned, mercifully, with guests either retiring to their rooms or to the dining room. But she wasn't about to let him get away with that jibe. 'There's only one solution to that. Champagne. The pop of a champagne cork always attracts attention.' She snapped her fingers to prove a point and a number of heads swivelled obligingly.

'You're tired and you're hungry. It'll go straight to your head.'

She sparkled her eyes at him. 'Promise?'

Was that what she was like with her lover? Silly? Flirtatious? Robert felt sickened by the way his mind was running, but he couldn't help it. Was that who she'd telephoned the minute he was out of the way in the bathroom? Had she called him to warn him not to come? Or just because she couldn't bear not to speak to him even for one evening?

Daisy flinched as something very like anger seethed back at her, heating the depths of Robert's dark eyes, but before he could say what was on his mind they were shown to a table in a secluded corner of the restaurant.

'Would you like to see the wine list, sir?'

Robert shook his head. 'Just bring a bottle of Bollinger.' He glanced briefly at the menu. 'And we'll have the wild mushroom pancakes followed by...' he paused momentarily, flicked a glance in her direction and smiled a little grimly '...roast duckling.'

'Excuse me!' Daisy declared the minute the waiter was out of earshot. 'I prefer to choose what I eat for myself.'

'You're an airhead, remember? Airheads like to be told what to do, what to eat. Believe me.'

'Oh, I do,' she retaliated. Then blushed.

'And they don't have the sensibility to blush.' And the wretch glowered at her as her colour deepened even further. 'But then, it's something of a lost art.'

Robert, despite everything that had happened, was beginning to enjoy himself. Their usual bantering conversational style had taken on an edge. A touch of danger. They were pushing one another in a way that had never happened before and it was oddly exhilarating. And the champagne would only add to the tension.

The waiter opened the bottle without making a fuss, and the cork breathed politely from the neck as a well-handled cork should. But nevertheless a number of people did turn and smile indulgently as they imagined some special celebration.

'So, you have your champagne,' he said, as they held their glasses. 'Now there has to be a toast.'

'Why?'

'It's traditional. It's what champagne was created for.'

'To the sale tomorrow, then. Successful bidding.'

He shook his head. 'Give it up, Daisy. It'll take more than a couple of giggles, a short skirt and a pair of high heels to turn you into the candyfloss kid.'

'Really? Oh, well, I'll try again.' She lifted the glass. 'Let me see, now, how about…to an undiscovered treasure at a knock-down price?'

'Not bad. Not quite silly enough, but not bad. Let's go for broke and make it a whole box full of treasures and no other bidders.'

She laughed out loud, attracting more attention. 'That's *very* silly.' Then she shrugged. 'But then so's the lottery. It doesn't stop George and I having a line between us every Saturday. To a box full of treasures and no other bidders, then.' And she touched her glass against his and sipped the champagne.

'What would you do if you won?'

'The lottery? Easy. I'd take a slow boat to China and another one to Japan. Then I'd hop on the QE2 to the States and visit all the great museums there.'

'You're not in a great hurry to get there?'

'Well, yes, but I'm scared of flying.'

'I don't believe it. I don't believe you're scared of anything.'

'Flying and earwigs.' And being in love with Robert Furneval. 'I'd buy something very rare and beautiful and give it to the Victoria and Albert Museum,' she rushed on. 'That way I wouldn't ever have to worry about it, but could go and look at it whenever I liked.' She paused. Then, because he was still looking at her as if he didn't believe her, she added, 'Buy you a new fishing rod. It's so long since you've fished, your old one must be broken. What about you?'

'I don't buy lottery tickets.'

'It doesn't matter. I'm never going to win; it's just a fantasy. So fantasise.'

Robert tried. He must want something, something so far out of reach that it would need lottery millions to buy it. But there was only one thing he longed for, yearned for. He hadn't known it, or particularly missed the lack of it, until this evening. But the ability to love one woman with all his heart and soul for the rest of his life…well, that wasn't something that money could buy.

'A tropical island,' he began a little desperately as Daisy's gaze seemed to burn into him, seeking out his secrets. 'A yacht.' Pathetic. He tried to laugh. 'A football club…' He saw the disappointment in Daisy's eyes. She thought him shallow. Well, she probably thought that anyway. He certainly couldn't tell her the truth. 'This isn't fair. You've had time to think about it.'

Robert was lying. For an instant, Daisy had seen something in his face, in his eyes, something he wanted so desperately that he couldn't put it into words. Or was afraid to.

She would have asked him what it was, but she knew that depth of hidden longing, knew he would pretend he didn't know what she was talking about. In his place, she would have done exactly the same. Instead she reached out and briefly touched his hand.

'Tell me another time,' she said, before turning to smile up at the waiter who had arrived with their pancakes. He served them, topped up their glasses and departed.

Usually their silences were restful things. Now the small sounds of silver against china seemed only to emphasise the quiet tension. He wasn't accustomed to awkward silences, not with Daisy.

What made it worse was that it wasn't a lack of something to say that constrained him. He had a heart full of words, all of them desperate to spill out and declare themselves. And if they did? She knew him better than anyone. She wouldn't take him seriously. Worse, because she knew him so well, she would be offended. And she had loved someone else for a long time.

Yet the touch of her fingertips burned against his skin and he wanted her to know that he cared.

'How about this?' he said. 'If I won the lottery I'd buy the fishing rights to a stretch of salmon river in Scotland and a comfortable cottage alongside it. And a pair of rods. One for you and one for me.'

Daisy had been pushing a mushroom around her plate, but now she raised her lashes and looked at him. 'You can't fool me, Robert Furneval. You just want me along to make the sandwiches.'

She thought she could see right through him. Well, maybe it was better if she continued to think that. 'You make great sandwiches. I love the baguettes you do with brie and stuffed olives. And the egg and bacon ones. And that thing you do where you wrap buttered bread around hot sausages...' His hand momentarily covered hers. 'Would you come?'

Her smile deepened and she twisted her hand beneath his and held it for a moment. 'Win the lottery and then ask me. But hurry. If I win first I'll be off on the first boat...'

'Well, isn't this sweet? Daisy and Robert holding hands. And champagne, too. Is there something you haven't been telling good old Monty?'

Daisy snatched back her hand. 'Monty! What on earth are you doing here?'

'Covering the sale, sweetheart,' he said, as he bent to kiss her cheek. 'I thought I'd see you here.' He glanced pointedly at Robert. 'I hoped I would. I never thanked you for all your help at my little do last weekend.'

'No problem,' Daisy said too quickly, too

anxious to change the subject. Robert could almost see the gossip columnist's antennae homing in on a story. 'It was a lovely party.'

'Nick didn't think so. The poor boy had the girl of his dreams snatched from right under his nose.' He turned. 'You're a sly one, Robert.'

He was too experienced at fishing himself to rise to the bait. 'I was just looking out for a friend.'

'Such devotion. Or maybe you've inherited your mother's eye for lovely things?'

Monty was so clever with words. However he replied it could be misconstrued, quoted out of context and given whatever spin the man fancied. 'I'm simply here in a cheque-signing capacity. My mother asked Daisy to look at some porcelain for her and possibly put in a bid for it.'

'Did she? It's nice work if you can get it.' He grinned at his own wit. 'Well, my trout is getting cold so I'll leave you young things to your hand-holding, but do join me in the bar later for a brandy. You can tell me all about it.'

Robert watched him return to his table. 'Oaf,' he muttered, when he was out of ear-shot.

'Monty's all right,' Daisy said. 'Just a bit silly. But what on earth is he doing here? He's not an arts columnist; he writes the gossip column.'

'Yes, well, this sale is the last gasp of a venerable dynasty with a whole wardrobe full of skeletons. Let's hope he'll be too busy rattling them to waste column inches on us.'

'Oh, but...' She began to laugh. 'He wouldn't!'

'He's a professional gossip, sweetheart. I wouldn't count on it.'

Robert was waiting for Monty when he entered the bar and he signalled the waiter to bring the brandy he'd ordered.

'On your own, dear boy?'

'Daisy's had a long day. I'm sure you'll have a chance to speak to her tomorrow if the dismantling of a dynasty doesn't keep you fully occupied.'

'No. The story's well documented and already written. I'm just looking for a few touches of bathos: the hordes picking over the bones. You know the kind of stuff.'

'You should find plenty here to fill your column.'

Monty picked up the brandy balloon and

swirled the pool of spirit at its base. 'If that's a hint that you'd prefer not to read about yourself, Robert—'

'I don't care about myself. I'm hoping you care enough about Daisy not to embarrass her.'

'I've already checked with the desk clerk, you know.'

'Then you'll know I booked a single room.'

'I also know that in an act of chivalry you offered it to a lady in distress. The young woman in Reception was very moved, but then there's nothing unusual about that. A smile from you would move mountains.' He sipped the brandy, then he sighed. 'I may be wrong, but I don't imagine you're sleeping in your car. Such a nasty night.' Robert didn't answer. Single beds wouldn't convince Monty. 'No. I didn't think so. You don't know a decent accountant who would do my taxes for me, do you? Someone who wouldn't charge the earth.'

Robert felt the tension ease from his shoulders. 'I'm sure I could find someone. For a friend.'

Monty nodded, apparently oblivious to any hint of sarcasm. 'Thanks. Shall we have another of these?' He summoned the waiter. 'Actually, you know, I'm not really surprised.'

'Not surprised about what?'

'About you and Daisy. Oh, two more brandies; he's paying.' He turned back to Robert. 'No, I was thinking about it over dinner. Well, you always go back to her, don't you? You have a little fling with some gorgeous girl but it never lasts. And then you're at a party or the theatre or somewhere and the girl at your side is Daisy. Again.'

'I'm not sure I'm following you.'

'Then you're not as smart as I thought you were.' And he lifted the glass the waiter put in front of him. 'Cheers.'

'Daisy?'

There was no answer, and in the small pool of light thrown by the table lamp across the space between the beds, Robert could see that she was asleep. She was lying on her side, her face pressed into the pillow, her hair a soft fuzz of curls, her body a gentle curve beneath the bedclothes.

He'd wanted to reassure her about Monty but there was no point in waking her. The morning would do. And he lowered himself onto the side of the bed, loosening his tie, unfastening his cuffs as he watched the gentle rise and fall of her breathing.

Monty was wrong. They were friends; that was all. They had always been friends. Even when she was a skinny kid and Mike had got so irritated when she'd tagged along he hadn't been able to resist that way she'd looked at him to back her up...

She still looked like a kid. Her soft pink lips were parted over the whitest of teeth and her skin had the peachy bloom of a baby. He reached out, wanting to touch it, stroke it, and for a moment his hand lingered a breath from her cheek. She looked untouched, brand-new, and he felt something deep inside him twist with pain. He didn't want anything bad to happen to her, knew that he would do anything in his power to prevent it.

His fingers curled back into his fist and he stood up, took himself to the bathroom to undress, horrified by the fact that while his mind was contemplating the lofty ideals of friendship, the rest of him appeared to be working on an altogether earthier agenda.

CHAPTER EIGHT

WEDNESDAY 29 March. I didn't sleep. Not one wink. I might have eventually drifted off—I was doing a pretty good job of pretending when Robert finally came to bed—but then he said my name and I nearly gave myself away. And he brushed my cheek. So gently. If he hadn't moved right then...

Robert was sleeping when Daisy finally crawled out of bed. No pretence about it.

He was lying on his back, one arm flung wide so that it hung over the bed, the sheets tangled around his waist. He looked so young, as if all the years since he had kissed Lorraine Summers had fallen away, and she longed to reach out, as he had in the night, and touch his face.

For a moment the tips of her fingers lingered over the hard line of his cheek, then she drew back. It would be better to let him sleep, dress without embarrassment, without him seeing her early-morning face. Not that he hadn't seen it before. But there was a whole world of difference between an early-morning kitchen and an early-morning bedroom, no matter how platonically shared.

She took her clothes into the bathroom, showered as quickly and quietly as she could. Then she made a single cup of tea and placed it on the night table beside him.

For a while she stood there, indulging herself in the pleasure of this unexpected intimacy. It seemed unlikely that she would ever have the chance again. He was laid bare for her. Shoulders, finely muscled arms, sculptured chest...all usually concealed by the civilising cloth of shirts made by hand in Jermyn Street.

'Goodbye...' The word whispered from her, then, as a tear squeezed beneath her lids, she bent and kissed his cheek. 'Goodbye.' Still he didn't stir. Well, there was no reason to wake him. And she turned and let herself quietly out of the room.

The phone woke Robert. He groped for the unfamiliar instrument, knocked over a cup, sending a cascade of cold tea over the night table, swore briefly before muttering an irritable, 'Furneval,' into the receiver.

*   *   *

In the dining room there was the quiet buzz of expectation, excitement as dealers and collectors gathered for breakfast. The thought of food almost choked her, but she needed juice, coffee, or she would never survive until lunchtime. She was beaten to the jug by Monty.

'Here, let me do that. Robert still sleeping it off?' he asked. Despite every attempt to appear cool, she blushed. 'Don't worry, I won't blab.'

'There's nothing to blab about, Monty.'

'No? Robert said that, too.' He smiled so sweetly that she was almost deceived into thinking that he believed him. 'But he was still prepared to buy me off.'

Buy? How much was a reputation worth these days? And was it her reputation or his own that he was concerned about? After all, the suggestion that he'd spent a night with Daisy Galbraith wasn't going to do much for his image. Hers, on the other hand, might take on some serious gloss. George would be delighted. Her mother would... 'You don't expect me to fall for that one, do you? You know perfectly well that Robert and I are just good friends—'

'*Really?*' He filled her glass with orange

juice. 'I didn't know it was as serious as *that*—'

'—and no one would have sent a dog out into last night's rain.' She put down the glass quickly as her hand began to shake, and began to sift through the yoghurts so that she wouldn't have to look at him. 'Not even you, Monty.' She picked a strawberry yoghurt, and because she knew deep down that running away was not the way to handle this, that if he thought she was trying to hide anything he'd never stop digging until he discovered the truth, she turned and looked him firmly in the eye. 'You can try to convince me that you're a black-hearted villain, but I know it's not true.'

'Oh, damn.' And he grinned like a naughty schoolboy. 'You won't tell Robert, will you? He's promised to have someone sort out my tax return.'

Well, that answered her question. A reputation in exchange for the services of an accountant. It was a good job she didn't have an inflated image of her own self-worth. She laughed and shook her head. 'Your secret is safe with me. I won't tell if you don't.'

He'd been dreaming. Before the telephone rang. He'd been dreaming about Daisy. After the crashing awakening, when he'd remembered, far too late, where he was and who he was with, he'd turned, expecting to see her snuggled down beneath the bedclothes like a little dormouse, unwilling to face a wet and chilly day. But the rain had stopped some time in the night and the sun was streaming in through a chink in the the curtains...

And her bed was empty.

Something made him touch his fingers to his cheek. It was damp, and when he looked at them there was the faintest smear of red. He recognised the colour. It was the same colour as the lipstick that Daisy had been wearing last night. And the colour broke his dream, so that he remembered that it had been of Daisy's lips against his cheek as she'd kissed him goodbye. No dream, then.

'Daisy?' The bathroom door stood ajar, her bag was zipped up and waiting by the door and her coat had gone. 'Damn!' He tossed back the covers and checked the bathroom anyway. Only then did it occur to him check his watch. It was nearly nine o'clock.

It had been hours before he'd dropped off to sleep, hours in which he'd lain listening to her soft breathing, hours during which he'd racked his brain in an attempt to get to the bottom of the mystery...

And the dear girl had left him to sleep. He rubbed his hand over his face. He'd needed it. He could still do with a solid eight hours. He stared at his reflection in the shaving mirror, the faint smear of red on his cheek. But his cheek had been wet. He touched his fingers to his tongue and tasted the unmistakable salt of tears...

Despite a buzz of nerves around her stomach, and a sickening certainty that she was about to make a complete and utter fool of herself, Daisy could at least be certain that she wouldn't let the gallery down by looking dowdy. Haggard, maybe. But not dowdy. At least it had stopped raining. The sun was shining and, since Monty had offered her a lift across the road to the Manor, she hadn't had to sully her expensive new shoes on the pot-holed drive.

Monty disappeared to look at the glories and the waste of the Warburys while she registered to bid, picked up her number and took one last look at the pieces she hoped to buy, including a casual walk past the bench with the boxed lots of kitchenware, barely glancing at the one she was interested in. When she went to take a seat in the marquee, Robert was standing just inside the entrance, waiting for her. He didn't look happy.

Robert saw her the moment she entered the huge temporary sales marquee that had been erected in front of the house. There were dozens of people arriving to stake their claim to the best seats, but among the men and women dressed for just another working day in clothes rubbed to a shine by countless salesroom benches she was impossible to miss.

Until a week ago, he'd have said he knew everything there was to know about Daisy Galbraith. He'd have been wrong. It was now quite obvious that he knew nothing about her. This woman, this totally stunning vision, was a stranger, a stranger who, under any other circumstances, he would have been breaking his neck to get to know.

It wasn't just the way her ridiculous duckling-yellow curls ruffled about her face. It was everything about her. The beautifully cut dark red suit, its thigh-skimming skirt demonstrating to anyone who cared to look that there was nothing wrong with her knees. Or her legs. What really confused him was the fact that he hadn't noticed that she was all grown up.

And it hurt, really hurt, that someone else had.

'You should have woken me,' he said, without preamble.

Daisy barely glanced at him, too busy surveying the marquee, rapidly filling with eager collectors. Or was it one collector that she was looking for? 'You looked so peaceful I didn't have the heart to disturb you. What's the problem? Did you miss breakfast?' she asked.

Her pertness irritated Robert, as did the sharp, sexy image which seemed so much more blatant in daylight. He didn't like it. He much preferred that soft, sweet girl he had watched over last night. A girl who would never have worn that shade of lipstick.

Yet the lipstick did it for him too. The thought of her leaning over him to kiss his cheek while he slept provoked a flood of heat that swept away the irritation. 'Breakfast was the least of my worries. Your sister rang you.'

'Sarah?' Her forehead crinkled into a little

frown. He wanted to smooth it away with the pad of his thumb, with his mouth... 'Why?'

He blinked. 'I haven't the faintest idea. She was in too much of a hurry to get off the phone and start spreading the news that I'd spent the night with you to leave a message.'

'Did you tell her that you did?' she said, a little catch of her breath doing ridiculous things to his heart-rate. 'Spend the night with me?'

Lord, but she was cool. When had she got this cool? 'No.' He hadn't. Not *with* her. 'She leapt to that conclusion when I answered the telephone. I was asleep when it rang, or I wouldn't have been so dim. That's why you should have woken me.'

That catch again, somewhere between a little shudder and a sigh. 'Oh, dear.' Or was she just finding it difficult not to laugh? 'I'm really sorry.'

'Why are you apologising?'

'Well, you seem upset, and I can see why. That kind of gossip won't do anything for your image.'

'*My* image?' What image? What the devil was she talking about? 'What about yours?'

'Ah, but I don't have an image, Robert.

Well, not that sort of image, anyway.' She appeared to give the matter some consideration. 'I suppose that kind of gossip might give me one, though. Look, can we find a seat before they're all taken? Over there, I think.'

For just the briefest moment Daisy had felt something akin to flying. The world would think Robert Furneval was her lover. It was the kind of dream she'd confided to her teenage diary...

It had never been pop stars for her. There had just been Robert, and one day he would look at her as if he saw the whole world in her eyes and everyone would understand that she was the only one for him. For a moment, a precious moment, she had thought it would happen.

But teenage diaries and real life had about as much in common as chalk and china. And because it wasn't ever going to be like that she had turned that little gasp into something more like laughter, made a joke of it and let it go.

Well, she was good at that; she'd been doing it all her life. Monty had believed her. So would everyone else. Robert, though, looked confused. Did he think she'd throw a vast wobbly and say she'd never be able to show her face in public again?

'Don't worry about it,' she said, and looped her arm through his. 'I'll call Sarah as soon as I get home. Explain what happened.'

'You expect her to believe you?'

'Why not? She'd do the same for a friend caught out in bad weather without a bed for the night.' A few minutes of clear thought and even Sarah would have to admit that the very idea of her little sister and Robert Furneval as a hot item *was* laughable. 'There wouldn't be any reason for me to lie.'

But what about her lover? How would he take it? In his shoes, Robert thought, he wouldn't be so sanguine. 'If the choice had been between sharing a room with Sarah and the deluge, I'd have taken the deluge.'

'She does talk rather a lot.'

'Well, I can promise you that she quite lost the power of speech this morning.'

They took the two remaining seats on the centre aisle, with Daisy on the outside so that she could see around a couple of hefty dealers, and the sale began.

'Is that it?' Robert asked, a couple of hours later, when she'd outbid the opposition

and taken the final item marked on her catalogue. 'Can we go and get some coffee?'

'Not quite.'

'But I thought that was all you wanted.'

'I'm hoping to get a box of kitchen china.'
His disbelief must have been easily read in
his face because she added, 'It's for a friend.'

What friend? 'I see. And how were you
planning to get it home on the train?'

She looked nonplussed. 'You're giving me
a lift, aren't you?'

'And if I hadn't turned up?'

'Oh. Well, I'd have managed somehow.'

Which answered any question about who
she'd phoned last night. He'd hoped to find
out when he paid the hotel bill, but Daisy
had got there before him. Clearly whoever
she was seeing had been warned to stay
away. 'Yes, I'm sure you would.'

'Look, why don't you go and get some
coffee? I won't be long.'

'No, I'll wait.'

'Then for goodness' sake stop twirling
your bidding number about, or you'll end up
with a box of old saucepans. Give it to me.'

He handed it over without demur and
watched while she bid in a desultory manner

for lot after lot of all kinds of kitchen junk without success.

'What on earth are you doing? Do you want this stuff or don't you?'

'At the right price.' She was tapping her bidding number against her knee as a number of small bids were made for yet another box of mouldy old china. She bid once, then again. Her rival, sitting a few rows back on the opposite side of the aisle, upped it again. Daisy appeared to lose interest, but then, just as the auctioneer was going to knock it down, she flipped up her number and at the same time slowly crossed her legs. By the time her opponent had got over the shock, the lot was hers.

'Come on. That's it,' she said abruptly. 'Let's go and sort out the paperwork.'

'I'm shocked.' Daisy turned to him. 'That was the most appalling exhibition of feminine mischief I've seen in my entire life.'

'I don't believe you. Besides, he'd been leering at me all morning.'

'What do you expect in a skirt up to your knickers and black stockings—?'

'They're tights. Stockings *would* have been tacky.'

'I'm glad you realise that.' He caught her

arm as she moved away from him. 'What are you up to?'

'Me? Dozy Daisy?' She handed him back his number. 'Pay your bill, Robert. That last lot was knocked down to you.'

Robert, about to argue, realised that he was missing something, and instead got out his chequebook and paid for a carton of filthy old kitchen china. 'Now what?'

'Go and fetch your car and then put that box on the back seat. Very carefully. I've just solved your birthday present problem.'

'What is it?' Robert had carried the box up to Daisy's flat and was now looking at the rather grubby and not particularly exciting piece of china that she was holding.

'A seventeenth-century Kakiemon dish. It's from Japan.'

'You're kidding.'

'No.' She gave little sigh and finally placed it carefully on the cloth with which she had covered the kitchen table. 'I couldn't be one hundred per cent sure until I'd held it,' she said, looking up at him. 'But that's definitely what it is.'

'Won't George Latimer want it?'

'George had his chance but he assumed

that I was hallucinating. Besides, there's no question of George having it. You bid for it, it's there in black and white on the receipt. You bid for it; you paid for it.'

'I thought that was an accident.' She didn't answer. 'You could have told me.'

'I might have been wrong, in which case I would have reimbursed you and sold on the china to a friend who runs a stall in a flea-market.'

Every aspect covered. 'While we're on the subject of paying for things, I have to split the hotel bill with you.' He would have settled it himself if she hadn't beaten him to it, but somehow he didn't think Daisy would respond very positively to any suggestion that he paid for the bed she'd slept in.'

'No need. Latimer's will pay. And they didn't charge any extra for you. I don't know why. The woman in Reception said that under the circumstances there was no charge.' She frowned. 'What circumstances?'

Robert placed the tip of his thumb against the space between her eyes. 'Don't frown.' Well, he had to distract her somehow. And then because the world seemed to shrink to that square inch of warm, vibrant skin, and because he'd been thinking about it all morning, he moved his thumb and kissed away the faint, puzzled crease. Her silky grey eyes widened and darkened, and for a heartbeat he had this feeling, deep down, that all it would take to change the world would be to say the three most precious words in the world. Unfortunately, there was no way on earth she would believe him. So instead he made his face smile. 'The wind might change.'

'Heavens.' Daisy's laugh was shaky and so was her hand as her fingers touched her forehead. He wanted to take that hand and put his arms around her and hold her. It would be the most shocking self-indulgence. 'Ginny's mother would kill me if I wasn't smiling on the wedding photos.' Her voice was shaking too. But she'd forgotten all about the hotel bill.

'I have to go.' He picked up the dish. 'Can you wrap this in something for me?'

'Um. Yes. No, leave it with me and I'll clean it, box it up for you. Men are hopeless at gift-wrapping.'

'That's why department stores offer the service. Are you sure you don't you want to keep it for yourself?'

'No. I love this stuff but I have no yearning to possess it. I was planning on giving it to Jennifer anyway, as a thank-you present. I just discovered she suggested George take me on.'

'Then it must be from both of us. Her birthday's on Sunday; will you come home with me? Unless of course you're busy?' She gave him a long look. 'What?'

She shook her head. 'Nothing. Only that's the first time you've ever asked me if I'm busy. You usually just assume I'll be available.'

Was he really that insensitive? Well, not any more. He'd taken Daisy Galbraith for granted for the very last time. He didn't understand why she'd let him get away with it for so long. 'I'm not assuming anything. I'm asking you because I want you to come with me. Will you?'

There was just a moment of hesitation before she said, 'I must admit I'd love to be there when Jennifer opens her gift.' Which put him in his place. 'But don't come knocking for me at seven-thirty. It's Ginny's hen night on Saturday and I'm anticipating a certain amount of remorse on Sunday morning.'

'We're hitting the town on Friday.'

'Well, don't get arrested. Ginny would murder you. Both of you.'

'Don't worry, I've never lost a bridegroom yet. And you—well, have a good time.' He paused in the doorway, remembering the last time they had stood on that threshold, the tender kiss that they'd shared. But that had been unpremeditated. This time it would be different, and as he hesitated, she brushed her cheek against his and closed the door.

This was getting to be a habit. Saying goodbye to Robert and feeling so weak that she couldn't let go of the doorknob. Her fingers shakily brushed against her forehead, where he had kissed away her frown.

She had been so sure just then, at the door, that he was remembering the way he had kissed her before. Ridiculous, of course. Why would he remember?

She closed her eyes and a deep moan escaped her. How would she ever forget?

The phone began to ring. She didn't want to speak to anyone, but she forced herself away from the door and picked it up, noticing that there were half a dozen messages waiting for her on her answering machine. No prizes for guessing who three of them

were. Her sister, her mother, George...
'Daisy Galbraith.'

'Daisy, I've been ringing and ringing.'

'Sorry, Mum. I've only just got back from
the Warbury sale.'

'Good trip, was it?'

'I got everything I went for. Is there something special, or is this just a chat? Only I'm
desperate for a shower.'

'No, nothing special. Sarah was trying to
get hold of you and I gave her the hotel number. I wonder if she found you?'

Her mother's attempt at being subtle could
teach a sledgehammer a thing or two. 'I had
a message that she'd rung. What does she
want? Do you know?'

'A babysitter for Friday night.'

'She rang me at Warbury for that?'

'It's desperate, apparently. The success of
her charity dinner depends on it. I've got a
committee meeting or I'd have driven up.'

'Oh, well, then.' She laughed, suddenly
back in control. 'It's clearly a crisis. Don't
worry, I won't let her down.'

'How was the visit to the hairdresser?'

'Surprisingly easy. He doesn't seem to
think I'll spoil the photographs.'

'Good, good.'

'If that's it, then?' It was cruel. Her mother was breaking her neck to know what had happened at Warbury but she was clearly having problems about asking the question outright. What was so difficult? Did you spend the night with Robert Furneval? Easy. And the answer. Not quite so clear cut. Yes and no. Mostly no. 'Mum?'

'Are you coming down at the weekend?'

'Well, Robert and I are going to see Jennifer on Sunday—'

'Oh?' It was a couldn't-quite-believe-her-ears kind of oh. 'Any particular reason?'

Anyone with a cruel streak would be enjoying this. Daisy was beginning to find it tiresome. 'It's her birthday. I found something rather special at the sale for her and Robert wants me to be there when he gives it to her.'

'I'll take her some flowers, then.'

'I'm sure she'll be delighted to see you. And I'll drop in and see you some time on Sunday. I'll bring the bridesmaid dress down with me...' how was that for a quick-thinking distraction? '...but I can't say what time.'

'Lovely.'

She pressed the playback button on the answering machine. 'Daisy, it's Sarah. I was so surprised by Robert answering the phone this morning that I completely forgot why I rang. I hope you know what you're doing. He's not exactly husband material and I always thought that you were a one-man sort of girl. Anyway, can you babysit on Friday night? Andy's going out on this bachelor thrash with Mike, I'm running a charity fundraiser for the local hospice and my regular girl has flu'. I'm desperate.'

That was it? Her mother had been so restrained she had nearly choked herself, and Sarah was being unbelievably restrained by her standards. She went on to the next message.

'Daisy, did you get it?' George asked. 'Was it Kakiemon?'

Oops.

The rest of the calls were hang-ups. Sarah or her mother, or even George, trying again, maybe. Or double glazing salesmen.

Robert flung his jacket over the nearest chair and headed for the phone. He was going crazy. He couldn't get Daisy out of his head. 'Mike? You've got to tell me who it is—'

'Hey, steady on. Calm down. What's the problem?'

'Daisy. She's the problem. She's wearing five-inch heels, skirts up to her thighs and black underwear. She's driving me crazy.'

'Black underwear?'

'Who is she seeing, Mike?'

'You're the one telling me what colour skimpies she's wearing. Besides, I don't remember saying that she was seeing anyone.'

'But you said—'

'I said she was *in love* with someone. Of course the difference may be too subtle for a man who thinks "love" is a four-letter word—'

'It is.'

'But there *is* a difference.'

'I see. You mean I've been running around like an idiot for nothing? She's not having an affair?' Robert tried to get his head around this unexpected turn of events while his system did a quick tour on a white-knuckle ride. There was no lover. Up. But she was in love. Down. 'Who?' he demanded. 'Who is she in love with? Do I know him?'

There was a long pause, and he could almost see the resigned shrug before Mike said, 'Yes.'

'Then for pity's sake put me out of my misery.'

'I can't. But I'll give you a clue. Elinor James.' And he chuckled. The wretch thought it was funny, did he? 'I'll see you on Friday.'

Robert dropped the receiver on the cradle and sank into a chair, rubbing his hands over his face. Daisy loved some unknown man so much that even though it was unrequited, unconsummated, she couldn't handle any other relationships. He wasn't sure whether that was better, or worse. A lover who was little more than a fantasy was unfair competition for any real flesh and blood man.

A fantasy couldn't forget birthdays or anniversaries because he wasn't ever expected to remember them. He couldn't say the wrong thing, or behave badly. There were no expectations for him to live up to. He moved through life being loved, but with no responsibility for that love. How did he know? Elinor James.

She'd been his fantasy once. Hell, she'd set the hormones jangling of every male in the school. Sixteen years old, silk blonde hair a yard long and with skin that looked as if it had been drenched in sunlight.

CHAPTER NINE

SUNDAY 2 April. Some time between remorse and lunchtime.

Ginny's sister certainly knows how to throw a party. And no one mentioned Robert. Not even Sarah. The words 'discretion' and 'valour' linked with her name seem an unlikely combination, but she managed not to bring the subject up at the party. Maybe she was afraid that if she did I might do something dreadful to her with Zorro's sword.

Daisy dressed for comfort rather than style. Comfortable trousers, a soft shirt, a favourite angora sweater.

'You look...'

'Comfortable?' Daisy offered, when words seemed to fail Robert.

'I was going to say cuddly, but it occurred to me that you might not appreciate that as a compliment.'

He was worried about offending her? 'You mean like a teddy bear?' she offered kindly.

'Do I?'

'It's the angora sweater,' she assured him.
'It's a bit like fur.'

'Can I check that out?' Before she could
stop him, Robert wrapped his arms around
her in a bear hug that trapped her arms and
held her so close that she was instantly
swamped in an emotive cocktail that over-
loaded her senses.

The cold touch of his chin, the slight rasp
of it against her temple. The mingled scents
of shaving soap and shampoo and toothpaste
that suggested he was not long from bed and
that while she had been standing beneath a
cool shower, hoping the water would pum-
mel some life into her limbs, a mile or so
away he had been doing much the same
thing. Her eyes, in the brief moment before
she slammed them shut, had a widescreen
close-up of his throat, the smooth skin beneath his ear and the thud, thud, thud of his
heartbeat came as a deep counterpoint to her
own. And she swallowed, hard.

'Mmm. Maybe you're right.' For a moment, as his arms loosened their grip, his
hands spread wide across her back, and for
a moment they stroked against the soft fluffy
wool. And Daisy knew why cats purred.

Then he stepped back, holding her for a moment at arm's length, his face creased in a frown of the most determined concentration. 'But I'll have to try that again without the sweater to be sure.' He smiled. 'It's entirely possible that you're cuddly without it. Are you ready?'

Not in a million years. In a heartbeat. Take your pick. 'For another hug?'

'Ready to go,' he said, and grinned. Inside her everything groaned. Groaned that she had fallen for such a cheap trick, groaned that she had wanted to fall for it. That was how he did it. A hug and a little teasing and that grin. That was how he swept girls off their feet. Well, she refused to be swept. 'We can try the hug again later, if you like,' he offered.

'No, thanks.' She handed him the box with the bridesmaid's dress. 'Here, put this in the car. I'll bring your mother's present.'

'How was the party last night?' Robert glanced at her as they sped through the Sunday quiet of Knightsbridge.

'We had a ball. And Zorro was a big success.' She realised she could have put that more delicately and yawned to cover her gaffe. 'Mike's party?'

'No complaints. Did Sarah mention Warbury?'

'I had the most dire warning on the answering machine. Nothing since. I think the combination of frozen margaritas and chilli must have numbed her tongue.'

'That'll do it every time. What did the warning consist of? Or shouldn't I ask?'

'I'd rather you forgot the whole incident.' And she yawned again. 'I'm sorry, Robert, but I can hardly keep my eyes open.'

'Put the seat back. Have a little snooze, if you like,' he suggested. 'You don't want to fall asleep over the birthday cake.'

She adjusted the seat, lay back and closed her eyes, glad of an excuse to avoid talking about the night they had spent at the Warbury Arms. She'd been trying very hard not to think about it ever since it had happened, with precious little success. She had this weird feeling that everyone knew but no one was saying anything, just holding their breath, waiting. For what, she hadn't the faintest idea. For someone to say April fool? But April Fool's Day had been yesterday...

She sighed, thinking about the way she had kissed him and said goodbye the morning of the sale. The tear had taken her by surprise, and she hadn't understood it at the time, but in the days since then the feeling had grown in her that the word had been more than a simple whisper into the dark. She had meant it. After the wedding she would go away. Leave London, leave Latimer's. Leave Robert.

It was time to turn her fantasies into reality. At least the ones that were in her power. China, America, Japan…

Robert parked the Aston in front of his mother's house, hooked his arm around the back of Daisy's seat and watched her sleeping. For a while back there, when she had so swiftly taken the chance to close her eyes and shut him out, he had suspected that she simply didn't want to talk to him, that she was hiding away from him rather than face what troubled her.

But beneath lids faintly dusted with a colour so vague that he would have been hard pressed to put a name to it, her eyes were moving as she dreamed. He wondered about Daisy's dreams. Were they happy?

As if to answer him, a tear welled up from beneath her lashes and then seeped over onto her cheek. It almost broke his heart.

'Oh, my darling,' he murmured, closing his hand, stroking her cheek with the back of his fingers in an attempt to comfort her. Another tear followed the first and, unable to bear it, he whispered her name. Her lids flickered over pupils dilated black and for a moment she blinked, uncomprehending. 'Come on, Sleeping Beauty,' he said, and he smiled to reassure her. He wished he could reassure himself. 'We're home.'

'What?'

'We've arrived.'

'Have we?' She shivered a little. 'I must have been dreaming. I thought I was in Japan.' As she struggled to sit up, Robert straightened the seat-back. 'I'm sorry,' she said, knuckling away the dampness around her eyes. 'I just meant to have forty winks.'

'Don't be. Sorry.' He tried to see in her face what had caused the tears, but awake she was far less vulnerable. 'If you can't sleep with a friend, who can you sleep with?'

'Oh, very funny,' she snapped. 'You should go on the stage.' She turned as Jennifer appeared at the front door, opened the door and without waiting for Robert swung her long legs from the car and swooped up the path. 'Happy birthday, Jennifer,' she said. And she hugged her.

There had been a time when she'd hugged him like that. A long time ago. When she was a girl and she hadn't seen him for ages, she would fling herself into his arms and hug him. When had those hugs turned into polite kisses to the cheek?

'I hate to break up the party, but I promised Mother I'd drop in with "The Dress". She's desperate to see it.'

'Do you want a hand with the box?'

'No, I can manage. Stay and help your mother with the washing up. But if I'm not back in half an hour please come and rescue me. Bring Major and suggest a walk. Flossie'll do the rest.'

'She's a lovely girl, Robert.' His mother joined him at the window as he watched her cross the green. 'And very bright. She should have kept the dish for herself, you know. Or sold it. She wants to go to Japan and China to study, and that costs money.'

Japan. She'd been dreaming about Japan. 'She wouldn't hear of it. She was going to give it to you anyway.' He turned to look down at his mother. 'Tell me about her.'

'You've known her most of your life. Longer than me.'

'I know, and I thought I knew her as well as anyone, but this last week or so... Well, it's as if I've met a complete stranger.'

'I see.' His mother's lips twitched into something close to a smile.

'You see? What?' He felt utterly frustrated. What was it that everyone else could see that he couldn't? 'What do you see?'

'Daisy hasn't changed, Robert. You have.'

'That's not true. You just see this girl.' He waved towards the window. 'This girl who wears shapeless trousers and old baggy jeans and no make-up—'

'I thought she looked very sweet in that sweater.'

'She looks utterly adorable in that sweater.' Sweet and sexy, and all he could think about was taking the damn thing off and doing the hug thing again and never stopping... He dragged himself back to the point. 'But you should see her when she's working. Skirts up to here,' he said, with a gesture that demonstrated exactly where the offending skirt had ended, 'dark red lipstick and black stockings—'

'Tights, surely? If the skirt is up to, um,

there?' He glowered at his mother. It might be her birthday, but that was no excuse for not taking him seriously. 'I'm sorry, Robert, but I don't understand what your problem is. You don't expect her to work in a West End art gallery dressed in jeans, do you?'

'No.' But he remembered the neck-to-toe clothes she'd been wearing when they'd last had lunch—about as alluring as a horse blanket. Nothing like that red suit. 'She never wears clothes like that when she sees me, whether she's working or not.' The little beaded handbag had been something of a giveaway, though, if he'd had the wit to see. With the horse blanket it had looked like something from a child's dressing up box. With the red suit it had been sharp and witty and sexy as hell.

'You'd like her to?'

'What? No!' Then he shrugged. 'Well, maybe.' He raked his fingers through his hair. 'I don't know what I want.'

'I think you probably do. You're just not ready to admit it.'

'There wouldn't be any point, would there? It's Daisy we're talking about. I wouldn't, couldn't, ever do anything to hurt her.'

'I know that.'

'Then you can see how impossible it is.'

'Because you think you're like your father? Incapable of commitment?' He shrugged helplessly. 'Why do you put so much store by the way he behaves? I left him when you were seven years old. I raised you. I have loved the same man all my life, although heaven alone knows he doesn't deserve it. You are my son, too.'

'Nature versus nurture? I'm nearly thirty-one years old and I've never yet met a woman who could hold my attention for more than a few weeks.'

'Except Daisy.'

He didn't deny it. 'Except Daisy.' Was that what Monty had meant about him always going back? 'Why didn't I realise the truth until it was too late?' Major bumped up against his leg and, glad of the distraction, he bent to rub his silky ears.

'It's never too late. Sometimes, though, it's too soon. Daisy was too young for a long time, Robert. When she was sixteen I was rather afraid she might do something very silly.' She was very still. 'I was afraid that *you* might do something very silly.' He looked up, but he didn't speak and she lifted hcr head a little. 'Do you remember that Christmas when you kissed her underneath the mistletoe?'

'The mistletoe.' His breath seemed to freeze in him as the elusive dream flooded his conscious mind and formed a solid image and he remembered. That was where he'd seen that look before, the sweet, sad yearning for something only to be guessed at, the look that turned a man's will to putty. 'I didn't realise anyone had seen.'

'I'd have said you were in another world...' She paused. 'Maybe I was wrong?'

'No.' He shook his head. 'What did you do?' His mother didn't answer. 'You did do something, I can see it in your face. What was it?'

'I called your father and asked him to take you skiing. And then, because she looked so miserable and I felt so guilty, I took Daisy to London for a few days to visit the British Museum, the V&A.' She looked up at him. 'Do you remember how she used to come flying round to the back door when she heard you were home from university?' He nodded. 'The year you graduated she'd been like a cat on a hot brick waiting for you to come home. She must have been out when you finally turned up, because Lorraine Summers beat her to it.'

'Lorraine?'

'She'd just come back from a year in Paris and she looked like a princess. She married a solicitor in Maybridge. She's got three children now.'

'I know who Lorraine Summers married,' he said. 'I was simply wondering what she had to do with this.'

'I imagine Daisy saw you kissing her. Or her kissing you.' She turned to look straight at him. 'She never came to the house again when she thought you might be home.'

'But that's ridiculous. I saw her all the time. I still see her all the time.'

'No, darling. You see her by appointment. You ask her to lunch, or to a party, or whatever it is you do in London. You don't see her by chance. Do you?'

'Well, no. But London is just a bit bigger than the village. When I'm home I see her all the time—'

'At home she has nothing to hide.'

'Hide?'

'At home she's the girl you've always known. You see her, darling, but only in the way she wants you to see her. Was she expecting you to turn up at Warbury?'

'No.' He felt hot with embarrassment at the way he had gone spying on her to Warbury.

'I thought not. I assumed you would simply telephone her and make the necessary arrangements. I never thought you'd go haring after her...' She smiled. 'If I'd thought about it, I would have arranged things rather better.'

'You couldn't have arranged things better if you'd thought about it for a month,' he assured her. 'It's a pity I didn't make better use of my opportunities. But I didn't go to Warbury because of the money. That was just an excuse.'

'Oh?' She began to stack cups onto a tray. 'Why *did* you go?'

'I was worried about her. Mike told me she was in love with someone. He made it sound very mysterious. I thought she might be having an affair with a married man.'

'Daisy?' She laughed. 'You mean you went racing off to Warbury in order to snatch her from the clutches of some self-serving man? Oh, darling, that's so sweet.'

'Not really. On closer inspection my case

of the galloping Galahads was the result of pure jealousy. I was so angry that someone else had taken something I treasured…something I had always thought was mine.'

'Daisy.'

'Yes, dammit, Daisy. Mike was giving me a prod; I can see that now. Making me think about her.' He raked his fingers through his hair. 'By heaven, he succeeded. I haven't been able to think about anything else for days.'

'Even though she's back in her cuddly sweater and her comfortable trousers?'

'Will you please stop talking about that sweater?'

'What is it about men and angora? No, don't answer that.' She laughed as she stood up and picked up the tray. Robert took it from her, carrying it into the kitchen. 'I always assumed, once she'd grown up at little, nature would take its course with the pair of you. But I hadn't bargained on Daisy. She's a girl with a mind of her own and she wasn't prepared to play. Wasn't prepared to be just one of Furneval's Fancies—'

'For heaven's sake!'

'Isn't that what they're called?' He didn't

answer. 'She's a till-death-do-us-part sort of girl, Rob.' She touched his arm. 'You're going to have to convince her that you're worthy of that kind of commitment.'

'Like Elinor James.'

'What, dear?'

'Nothing. Just something Mike said.' Elinor James could have had any boy in the school at her feet. He had been no different, but he hadn't been prepared to put up his hand and say, Me too. He'd kept his distance and his pride. For a while his friends had kept a book on how long he could hold out. Then, one day, they'd begun to bet on how long it would be before she asked him out.

How many of his friends were watching him now? Waiting to see how long it would take him to realise that Daisy was there...

Monty, certainly. He'd said as much. Monty spent his life watching people make fools of themselves; he saw relationships form and disintegrate even before the people involved knew what was going on.

Mike, of course. But Mike had never said anything; he understood him too well. He would probably never have said anything except, giddy with a happiness that he wanted everyone to share, he hadn't been able to resist throwing out a hint. Or had it been a veiled challenge? Had Mike realised all it would take would be a little plain old-fashioned jealousy?

He dragged his hand over his face, saw his mother was looking at him, waiting... His mother knew. Maybe even Sarah knew. Suddenly it was all so clear, so obvious, that he wondered if he was the only person in the world who hadn't been able to see the truth.

Or maybe he had shut it out, buried the memory of a young girl who had spirited away his heart and kept it. 'You were right, you know. About Daisy. But wrong, too. I knew that she was too young. Lorraine was simply a distraction. I've been distracting myself for years, waiting for her to grow up. And when she did, I was—'

'Distracted?'

'How on earth am I ever going to convince her to trust me? To take me seriously?'

'Do you want her to?'

'Oh, yes.'

She patted his arm. 'Maybe a walk will clear your head. Take Daisy through the orchard and perhaps you'll recapture some of that mistletoe magic.'

* * *

'You've brought the dress!' Margaret Galbraith took the box from her and carried it upstairs. 'Oh, Daisy, it's lovely,' she said, lifting it from the tissue. 'Put it on. I want to see what it looks like.'

'It won't look right without the shoes and the hair,' she warned.

'I can imagine those. Oh, my goodness, look at this.' She picked up the lacy bra that provided some special effects in the cleavage department.

'Yes, well, I needed a little help. It's that sort of dress.'

She'd known how it would be, but anything that distracted her mother from what happened at Warbury was to be welcomed. She pulled off her sweater and blouse and stepped out of her trousers, but she wasn't stripping off in front of her mother. It was going to be bad enough without that. 'I can manage. I'll give you a call when I'm ready.'

'No, come down. Dad will want to see too.'

As she eased herself into the exquisite lace underwear, Daisy felt about six years old, trying on a pretty new frock and going downstairs to show her daddy. The more things changed, the more they stayed the same.

She stepped into the dress, fastened it, fluffed up her hair. But it wasn't modelling the dress that bothered her, it was the inevitable look of discontent on her mother's face. The fact that she would never wear it as well as her sister could have done.

'Daisy?' Her mother was getting impatient.

'I'm just coming. You've shut Flossie in the kitchen, haven't you?' Reassurance was swift, and there was nothing for it but to lift the softly draped white voile skirt and go downstairs. For a moment neither her mother nor father said anything. 'Well?'

'You look lovely, Daisy. Doesn't she, Margaret?' her father said, encouragingly.

'Well. I thought the yellow would be a disaster, but, no... The bodice is very small, very neat, and the white skirt is very light and pretty. The idea is charming. Of course on the other girls, with their dark hair, it will be much more striking, but even so, with the right make-up... Turn around.'

Daisy obediently turned. Robert was standing in the doorway. He was looking at her in a way that she couldn't fathom. No teasing smile, no silly grin, just the kind of look she'd always dreamed of. Intense, deep, soul-searching. It seemed like for ever before he broke the silence.

'Ducklings, it seems, are getting more swan-like every day.' Then, realising that everyone was staring him, 'The back door was open. I've left Major in the mud room.' Then he slapped his hand to his forehead. 'Oh, no, don't tell me it's unlucky for the best man to see the bridesmaid before the wedding.'

Her father began to laugh, her mother spun around and glared at him and he immediately stopped.

'I'd better go and change,' Daisy said.

She had to wait for Robert to move aside. He took his time. 'You needn't have worried about the colour, you know.' His face was smiling now, the way it always did when he was teasing, but his eyes were still dark and intense and full of secrets. 'It matches your hair perfectly.' And he flipped a curl. Teasing. But it was teasing for the benefit of their audience, not for her.

'Swans, indeed.' Her mother, affronted, bustled her out of the room and followed her up the stairs, as if afraid that Robert might take it into his head to offer to help with the hooks and eyes. 'Don't let him turn your head with that silver tongue of his, my girl.'

Daisy tugged at the hooks. 'He never has before.'

'He's never tried before,' she said, her voice heavy with meaning. 'He's just like his father.'

'I didn't know you'd ever met Robert's father.'

'I haven't, but I've seen a picture of him.' She put the dress on a padded hanger. 'Divorced for more than twenty years and poor Jennifer's still got a photograph of him by the side of her bed. She's a good-looking woman, but I've never even seen her with another man. Of course, that combination of good looks and charm is absolutely fatal. There ought to be a law against it.' She hung the dress in the wardrobe, busied herself draping it with the tissue paper. 'Robert looks just like him, you know.'

'You said.'

'Behaves like him, too. I suppose it's a case of like father, like son.'

'Mum...' She was going to explain, reassure her mother that nothing had happened at Warbury. Instead she heard herself saying, 'I'm twenty-four. And I've known Robert for ever. I trust him. He wouldn't do anything to hurt me.'

For a moment her mother looked startled. 'I know that.' Then she sighed. 'I know that. I'm sorry. I'm lecturing you as if you were still a child. But then, to me, you always will be. All of you. Sarah says I treat her like an infant, too...telling her how to bring up the children as if she isn't the most capable mother. But once the nest is empty what do you do?'

'Live the rest of your life. Enjoy yourself. Take a holiday.' Daisy put her arms about her mother and held her. 'Next week the wedding will be over and you'll be feeling horribly flat. It's April, Mum. Ask Dad to take you to Paris. Or book the tickets your-self and take him. You don't have to be young, or newly married, to take a honey-moon.'

Flossie was whining with excitement in the kitchen, and when Daisy opened the door she practically threw herself on Major before bounding out of the door, heading towards the river. Robert whistled to her and turned the other way. 'It'll be muddy,' he said.

'It usually is. Where are we going?'

'This way.'

Daisy glanced at him, about to respond with something sarcastic, but he seemed so deep in thought that she left it and they walked on in silence for a while.

'Flossie!' The spaniel, pushing her way through the hedge, finally caught his attention. 'For goodness' sake, that dog is the worst behaved animal—'

'Hey, don't be so tense.'

Robert glanced at her. 'No. I'm sorry.' He stopped by the kissing gate into the old orchard next to the church and swung it open for her.

'It's too early for blossom,' she said, when he stopped to look up into the branches of one of the old trees.

'I'm not looking for blossom; I'm looking for mistletoe. It grows on apple trees. Well, on this apple tree, anyway.'

'Not in April.'

'It's always there. It's just that when you can't see it, it's easy to forget.' She lowered her gaze from the branches. Robert's face was shadowy, his eyes unreadable, but she could read his thoughts as clearly as if they were her own.

'I think we'd better go. Where are the

dogs?' As she began to turn, he reached out for her, turned her gently to face him. 'Do you remember the Christmas you were sixteen, Daisy?' She remembered. 'When I kissed you underneath the mistletoe?'

She swallowed. 'Yes.' Her first kiss. So sweet, so special. She'd had the most vivid reminder only a few days ago.

'I cut it from this tree.' He looked up. 'I'm sure it was this tree.' She didn't know what to say, except that without him mistletoe was a pointless custom. And she couldn't say that.

'They're going to fell the orchard this year.'

He wasn't to be diverted. 'Do you remember what I said?'

A little spark of something like anger seemed to ignite inside her. How would she ever forget what he said to her that night?

'Do you?' she demanded.

'I'd forgotten.' His hand moved against her shoulder in a tender caress. Gentling her, soothing her, as if he understood how much his admission would hurt. 'I knew there was something. I think I must have blocked it out, but I knew there was something precious, something special, just out of reach. You know how it is when you wake and you know you've been dreaming and that, more than anything, you want to be dreaming again, but you don't know why.' She knew. Oh, yes, she knew. 'The memory of it is like a will-o'-the-wisp, always there, but always slipping away down the side alleys of the mind before you can catch hold of it.' His hand moved to tilt her chin so that she had no choice but to look at him, or close her eyes. She closed her eyes. 'I said... "I'll wait for you."'

She felt his breath close to her cheek, the merest touch against her lids, and like the sun opening a flower his touch loosened the traitorous words from her tongue. 'I didn't want to wait,' she said, and because hiding was no longer an option, either from him or from herself, she opened her eyes.

'No.' It was shadowy beneath the tree; the sun was low and everything was tinged with a luminous pink so that the leaves above them looked like blossom. 'Neither did I. But you were too young. If I'd been sixteen too, well, that might have been forgivable...'

This was unforgivable. Making her remember. It had taken months, years to forget the heartache, to pretend to herself that it had been nothing more than an unaccustomed glass of wine that had gone to her silly girlish head and made them both say things that in the cold light of day they'd hoped would be forgotten. He had forgotten. She never could. This was like tearing her heart in two all over again.

He looked up again, then smiled. 'Will you kiss me beneath the mistletoe one last time, Daisy?' *One last time? That sounded so very final.* 'Before they cut down the tree.'

'I...' Can't. Mustn't. Shouldn't. The words wouldn't come and he took her silence for assent.

It took a while. His lips hovered tantalisingly close and she tilted her head a little to one side and waited, as eager as her sixteen-year-old self had been all those years ago. He drew back a little, one corner of his mouth lifted in a self-conscious little smile. He tried again, and again, an inch from her lips, he paused. It was sweet and silly and she began to giggle.

'Shh. This is serious. We're kissing each other for the very last time beneath this apple tree.' His arm slid about her, his hand spread across her waist, keeping her still. Keeping her close. 'Laughing is not allowed.'

'No.' She tried to straighten her face, but it wouldn't co-operate. Being kissed by Robert was never going to be serious. Never.

And without warning all desire to laugh evaporated. Like father, like son. This wasn't funny. It was almost certainly the stupidest thing she had ever done. Bar none.

'Robert, no—' But her protest came too late. He brushed the words from her lips, erased them with a touch that was like a feather against her mouth, once, twice, three times in a tender evocation of that long-ago kiss.

Then he drew back a little, the teasing smile back in place. 'It's all coming back to me now.'

'Robert—' She grasped helplessly at the chance to escape before she betrayed herself beyond all recall.

Maybe he would have let her go. Maybe not. She was no longer too young, he was at a loose end and maybe, just maybe, she would have been foolish enough to believe his silver words... But Flossie, excitable and silly and covered in mud, came hurtling through the trees, flinging herself at them.

And somehow, in the confusion, the sponging down of their clothes, a cup of her mother's tea, normality gradually reasserted itself.

CHAPTER TEN

SATURDAY 8 April. Ginny and Michael's wedding day. Very early. Robert came over a while ago and I heard him and Mike take the dogs out. He usually tosses a little gravel up to my window to see if I want to tag along, but not this morning. Maybe it was a 'man' thing.

Not that I would have gone with them. I don't have time for a walk. After that kiss in the orchard nothing is ever going to be the same. But I won't…I will not… Even if it does mean I have to leave the country to avoid temptation.

All I have to do is get through today. With any luck Robert will have forgotten that he asked me to have lunch with him and won't discover I've bolted back to London until it's too late.

The church looked glorious, the lych-gate garlanded with yellow and white flowers entwined with evergreens, every pew-end decorated with matching ribbons and glossy green ivy. And Ginny so beautiful...

Daisy knew that crying at weddings was acceptable, but this lump in her throat, the solid ache that was like a stone in her heart, surely that was more than convention demanded?

If only Robert hadn't worn that silly yellow waistcoat. She had prepared herself for everything but that. He'd done it for her, and as he half turned, half smiled, she knew she was expected to indicate in some small way that she appreciated the effort.

She tried. She really tried. She made every effort to put out a quirky smile, all eyebrows and mouth so that he would know that she'd duly noted the trouble he'd taken to amuse her.

But the lump in her throat was doing something to her mouth, and if she quirked her brows, the tears would spill over and spoil the careful make-up which had been applied by a woman brought all the way from London for the purpose. That would be the most dreadful waste.

So instead she looked at the neat little posy she was carrying and pretended not to see.

Japan. She hung on to the promise of Japan. Her bag was packed, her ticket booked. Dear George. He'd done far more than simply let her go without a murmur about the inconvenience. He'd contacted friends, organised somewhere for her to stay until she could decide what she was going to do. Maybe he was glad to let her go; he hadn't been entirely happy about the dish incident. She didn't have the instincts to be a dealer, he'd said; she should stick to scholarship. Maybe he was right.

All Sunday night Robert's kiss had kept her awake. She'd tossed and turned but all she'd been able to think of was her mother saying *'like father, like son'* and *'poor Jennifer'* and imagining herself, thirty years from now, having people say *'Poor Daisy. She was in love with Robert Furneval, but he was just like his father...'*

Then on Monday morning she'd walked into the gallery and George had told her that they'd had a little win on the lottery. Ten pounds. Five pounds each. And she'd thought about the 'this year, next year, some time, never' fantasy that she and Robert had played over dinner at Warbury. It had seemed like fate. She'd had a win on the lottery. The amount didn't really matter; she had some money that her grandfather had left her—Mother always referred to it as her 'dowry'. Well, she wouldn't be needing a dowry, and it was time to choose between the dreams.

She glossed over the following hour. She wasn't proud of that. But George had offered her his handerchief and listened as it had all poured out of her, all the pain, all the dammed-up passion, all the love. Then he'd made her green tea from his special caddy, and while she'd sipped it through the hiccups he'd made some calls to friends. Then he had sent her home to organise herself.

And so tomorrow she would be on her way to Tokyo, to a new life discovering the mystery and beauty of another culture. It was dream-come-true time.

Then Robert had to go and wear a yellow velvet waistcoat and destroy the illusion.

Wrong dream.

Through the swimmy veil of tears she saw Michael kiss Ginny, and then, somehow, Robert was holding her arm and they were following the newly-weds into the vestry to sign the register. Robert witnessed the entry and the pen was passed to her to do the same.

She sniffed. 'My hand's all shaky.'

Robert produced a handkerchief, tilted her chin and then gently dabbed at her eyes so that the make-up wouldn't smudge. Then, for just a moment, he held her, and she closed her eyes and let the comfort flow over her. 'There now, big breath.' That was shaky, too, but it did the trick and Robert handed her the pen, his eyes not teasing but sympathetic, as if he knew exactly how she was feeling.

Ridiculous.

But when the deed was done, the formalities concluded, he retrieved her fingers and kept them comfortingly tight in his as they lined up behind the bride to leave the vestry and follow the newly married pair out of the church and into a new life.

Confused, Daisy glanced back at the other bridesmaids, her look apologetic; this wasn't how it was meant to be. Robert, however, appeared oblivious to the three exquisite brunettes who lined up behind them.

Once at the reception, they tried, they really tried to catch his attention, to lure him into quiet corners, but even the wonderful Victorian conservatory proved no temptation. Robert was polite and charming, to be sure, but no more than that to the dozens of aunts, cousins, grandmothers and every other variety of female relation to whom he was introduced.

For once in his life he wasn't flirting. It made her nervous.

The speeches were done, the bride and groom were changing and Robert had disappeared. She took the opportunity to slip out onto the terrace, get away from the noise and the laughter. A few more minutes. Once Ginny and Mike had left, she too could escape.

'Cast not a clout till May is out...' Not yet. Not quite yet. Robert crossed the terrace, taking off his morning coat. 'And I'll bet any amount of money you're not wearing any clouts beneath that dress. Whatever they are. Here.' He slipped the coat about her shoulders.

It was warm from his body and she pulled it around her. 'Thanks. It's a bit noisy in there.'

'It's very noisy,' he said, leaning his arms against the balustrade. 'In fact it's a great wedding. If you like that kind of thing.'

'Mmm.'

'Well, that was...noncommittal. I expected to be read the riot act for speaking heresy at the nuptial feast.'

'I'm sorry to disappoint you, but weddings don't do a lot for me. Call me unromantic, but I take the view that it would be a lot less trouble just tearing up fifty-pound notes in a force nine gale.'

'You could be right. What will you do?'

'Me?'

'When you marry.'

She turned and looked at him for a moment and then looked away again. 'I'm not going to get married. I'm going to be a distinguished oriental scholar and travel the world.'

'Starting with Japan.' For a moment, for just a heartbeat, she thought he had discovered her secret. It had to be a secret. He had to think he had time. She knew Robert. Had seen him at work. Warbury had given him ideas, reminded him of unfinished business, and the scene in the orchard had been the opening salvo in a campaign to get her into his bed. But for Flossie... 'Humour me,' he said, when she didn't answer. 'If you did decide to marry, who would you want to be there?'

Relief made her garrulous. 'Oh, I think

two people somewhere very quiet, very peaceful, very beautiful would be all the company that was necessary.'

'No bridesmaids, then.' He looked down at the waistcoat. 'No yellow velvet.'

'Not even a best man,' she assured him. Especially not a best man.

'I'm sold. Will you marry me?'

She made a noise that might have been a laugh. Just. 'Haven't you got something very best-mannish to do, Robert? Like tying balloons and old shoes to the getaway car?'

'It's done.'

'Well, what about seducing a bridesmaid, or something?'

He glanced back at her. 'Are you volunteering?'

'Robert...'

'Robert! Daisy! There you are.' Sarah emerged from the ballroom looking slightly dishevelled from the dancing and with a silly grin plastered over her pretty face. Then she looked from her sister to Robert and she stilled, seeming to sense that she had interrupted something important. 'I'm sorry, but Ginny and Mike are just leaving.'

'We'll be right there.' Daisy slipped off Robert's coat and gave it back to him. Then she shivered and walked quickly inside to join the crowd gathering at the foot of the ornate staircase. Ginny was standing at the top, bouquet in hand, and as she saw Daisy she grinned and turned her back before tossing her flowers over her head into the waiting guests.

Someone behind her caught them, and as heads turned there was an expectant hush. Robert. He'd come in behind her and the flowers Ginny had aimed in her direction had instead been caught by him.

It was the moment for wit, the sharp, telling remark that would make everyone laugh. But wit was beyond her, and when Robert offered them to her with the slightest of bows she could do nothing but take them and submit, in silent misery, to the gentle, 'Ah!' that swept through the room.

It could only have lasted a few seconds, but it seemed like for ever before everyone surged after Ginny and Mike, and with a last flurry of flashes from half a dozen cameras, waved them away down the drive.

'I don't understand. How can there be a problem?' As if flying wasn't harrowing enough. 'My ticket was confirmed last week.'

The woman behind the check-in smiled. She was clearly used to irate passengers and had done the course about keeping her voice low, her expression positive. 'We tried to contact you yesterday, but there was no reply from your number. And there isn't a problem, as such. We've found you a seat on another flight leaving within half an hour.' Another flight going via Delhi, with a twenty-four-hour stop-over. Daisy was not happy. She'd booked a direct flight to avoid unnecessary take-offs and landings. 'We have upgraded you to first class,' the woman continued swiftly, 'and there will be a complimentary sight-seeing excursion...'

There was no point in getting angry. It wasn't this woman's fault that some computer had messed up. She phoned her mother to tell her the change of plan. 'Tell George, will you, Mum? He'll have to let people know at the other end.'

'Of course. Send me a postcard of the Taj Mahal.'

'The what?'

'And, darling...be happy.'

Before she could answer, her mother had

rung off. She'd been unusually emotional when they'd said goodbye. Daisy had put it down to the wedding, to the champagne, but even now she'd sounded on the edge of tears...

The Taj Mahal?

She hadn't realised that her mother knew India that well. Had she even mentioned that she was stopping over in Delhi. She'd just said, Oh, well... It was probably just one of those things you said to someone visiting India. Send me a postcard of the Taj Mahal.

She brightened a little. If that was the complimentary excursion on offer, she'd definitely be taking it.

She settled herself in her seat at the front of the first-class section and took out her book. She hated this. The minutes before take-off, the slow taxiing to the end of the runway, the winding up of the engines...

'Will you please ensure that your seats are in the upright position and your seatbelt is securely fastened...?'

She knew it was silly. She knew the statistics. More people died falling out of bed... But still she clutched at the armrests and closed her eyes.

Someone took the seat next to her. She

heard the click of the seatbelt. She knew she must look like an idiot, but nothing could make her open her eyes until they were safely off the ground.

Nothing but a cool hand covering her own. Robert's voice saying, 'It's true, then.' Her disbelief was more powerful than her fear and she swung round.

'Robert?' She could see it was him, he was holding her hand, but she still didn't believe it.

'I thought you were going to take a boat?'

'I couldn't afford it.'

'But I heard you'd won the lottery.'

'Ten pounds. Well, five pounds, actually, George and I share…' She stopped. It wasn't important. 'What are you doing here?'

'Holding your hand. Going to India for the bank. Asking you to marry me. Not necessarily in that order. I have a week before I need to start work.'

The plane began to move but Daisy didn't even notice. The surge of longing for it to be true was choking her. 'You're going to India? What an amazing coincidence.'

'I think putting this down to coincidence would be stretching the boundaries of common sense beyond any natural limit. Will you marry me, Daisy?'

This couldn't be true. 'I'm going to Japan.'

'India's on the way.'

'Only if you take the slow plane. How long will you be there?'

'As long as it takes. You're running away, Daisy. Hiding from me again.' The plane stopped, turned. 'We've both been hiding, but it's time to stop. Will you marry me?'

The noise of the engine built up. 'You're not the marrying kind, Robert.'

'You've been listening to gossip. But then, so have I.'

'You've been living it. I understand where you're coming from, Robert. You're thinking, Hell, this is *Daisy*. Now I've seen her legs I want to add her to my collection. But I can't just have a little fun with Daisy because...well, *because*...'

'Because Mike would never speak to me again? Or my mother would disown me? Or even, heaven help us, your mother would use her rolling pin for something other than pastry...' She said nothing. 'You see? I know where you've been coming from, too. It took a while, and I needed some help.'

'Help?' Who from? How much worse could this get?

'Mike gave me a prod. He said you'd been in love with someone—well, for ever. I spent days trying to find out who was giving you a hard time... I was going to deal with him...'

'Oh.'

'What *is* the password for your computer?'

The conversation was surreal. 'Rabbit.'

'Rabbit?'

'I call my computer Peter...' He shook his head as if he couldn't believe it. 'Is it important?'

'Apparently not.' His grip on her hand intensified. 'Did I mention that Monty knew? He pointed out how you were the one girl I never tired of, always went back to.'

'Monty said that?'

'It surprised me too. But it's what he does, my love. Watches people make fools of themselves as they fall in and out of love.'

'This gets worse.'

'I haven't finished.' She groaned. 'My mother told me that you saw me kissing Lorraine Summers, and that's when you began avoiding me. You were far too young for a proper relationship, Daisy. And I was far too young to know how to wait. Please marry me, Daisy.'

It was getting harder to ignore his question. But she would try. Just a little longer. 'Does your mother know? That you're here?'

'They all know. Come on, Daisy. You know you want to—'

'Stop it!' She put her free hand to her head. 'Stop it!' The plane was shaking. 'I need to think.'

'No, you don't. You're on this plane because you're running away again. I'm telling you that I won't let it happen.' He took her other hand. 'You've always had the best of me, Daisy. I've never lied to you. I'm not lying to you now. I love you. I've always loved you. I'll wait if I have to prove it, but I think we've both waited long enough.' He released her hand, captured her face and held it so that she couldn't look anywhere but at him, couldn't avoid eyes that promised her his heart on a plate. 'Will you, please, please, marry me?'

They were rocketing along the runway; her heart was pounding with the explosive beat of the engines. Risk. Life was a risk. But she knew Robert. He never lied; he never cheated. He might be like his father, but he was like Jennifer too. His heart, once given, would never belong to anyone else. And the truth was as bright as the sunlight above the clouds. They were flying; her heart was flying.

'Champagne, sir, madam?'

He was looking at her. 'Champagne, Daisy?'

One long shuddering breath and then she was lost. 'Yes. Oh, yes, please.' But, as he handed her a glass, 'No. Wait. I don't understand. How did you know I'd be on this plane? I should have been flying direct...'

Robert touched his glass to hers. 'To computers, bless them, for always being there to take the blame. And a travel agent with a soul that was pure romance.'

'Are you telling me that you *fixed* this?'

'With a little help from some friends. After George had fixed everything up for you he began to wonder if he'd done the right thing, so he called my mother for advice. And because she knew how I felt, she called me.'

'Robert, people are expecting me—'

'People have been warned that you might be delayed,' he said gently. 'It's your choice. Marry me, go on to Tokyo next week and I'll join you as soon as I can. Or stay with me and we'll go on together. I'll take a sabbatical to study the way the Japanese do things while you do whatever it is you want to do.'

'You've got it all figured out, haven't you?'

'I'm a banker. Figuring is my job. But I have to tell you that it's been a tough week.'

'So why didn't you say something before I left?'

'Because there was too much going on. Too many distractions.' He lifted her hand, kissed the palm. 'And because I thought I was going to need every minute of eight and a half hours without muddy dogs, or sisters with terminally bad timing—eight and a half hours with you securely fastened into a seat beside me and no escape—to talk you round. I over-estimated by about eight hours and twenty-five minutes.'

'You just caught me at a weak moment.' Then she grinned. 'It was a terrific cure for fear of flying, though.' She turned her hand to clasp his, touching it to her cheek. 'I guess that does it for me. I'll have to stay with you, Robert, if only to have you there to hold my hand on take-off.'

* * *

Daisy wore a red and gold wedding sari, Robert a cream tropical suit. The paperwork had been dealt with. The officials. The legal stuff. Now they sat together, looking at the world's most beautiful monument to love and its perfect reflection in the still water, holding hands and considering the future.

Then, as a huge white moon rose into the blackness of the sky, Robert turned to Daisy. 'I love you,' he said. 'I will always love you.'

And Daisy said, 'I love you. I have always loved you.'

He touched the exquisitely worked gold and diamond wedding ring she wore for him before lifting her hand to his lips. 'The waiting, my love, is over.' And then he took her in his arms and kissed her.

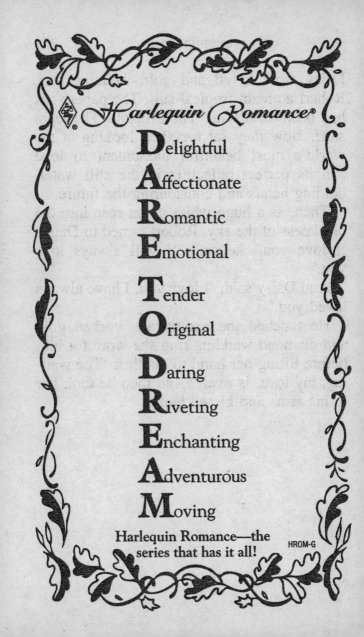

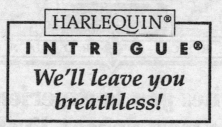

HARLEQUIN SUPERROMANCE®

...there's more to the story!

Superromance. A *big* satisfying read about unforget-
table characters. Each month we offer
four very different stories that range from family
drama to adventure and mystery, from highly emotional stories to romantic comedies—and
much more! Stories about people you'll
believe in and care about. Stories too
compelling to put down....

Our authors are among today's *best* romance writ-
ers. You'll find familiar names and
talented newcomers. Many of them are
award winners—and you'll see why!

If you want the biggest and best
in romance fiction, you'll get it
from Superromance!

Available wherever Harlequin books are sold.